MATTHIAS

MATTHIAS

A NOVEL

Elsie J. Larson

1817

Harper & Row, Publishers, San Francisco

New York, Grand Rapids, Philadelphia, St. Louis
London, Singapore, Sydney, Tokyo, Toronto

MATTHIAS: *A Novel.* Copyright © 1990 by Elsie J. Larson. All rights reserved. Printed in the United States of America. No part of this book may be used or reproduced in any manner whatsoever without written permission except in the case of brief quotations embodied in critical articles and reviews. For information address Harper & Row, Publishers, Inc., 10 East 53rd Street, New York, NY 10022.

FIRST EDITION

INTERIOR DESIGN BY RICHARD KHARIBIAN

Library of Congress Cataloging-in-Publication Data
Larson, Elsie J.
    Matthias, a novel.

    1. Matthias, Saint, Apostle—Fiction.   2. Bible. N.T.—History of Biblical events—Fiction.   I. Title.
PS3562.A7522M38   1990   813'.54   89-45931
ISBN 0-06-064951-8

90 91 92 93 94 HAD 10 9 8 7 6 5 4 3 2 1

This edition is printed on acid-free paper that meets the American National Standards Institute Z39.48 Standard.

*With thanksgiving and much love
this book is dedicated to my husband,
Richard*

MATTHIAS

One

A groan of pain and the whisper of running bare feet snapped Matthias to attention. He froze, trusting the night to conceal him as well as it hid violent men. In Jerusalem in the dark of the moon, thieves robbed at will.

In the flicker of a nearby gate torch, a black alley sliced between the high walls of two great houses. Matthias approached it warily and listened. A low moan confirmed the direction.

He slipped his dagger from his girdle and stepped to the mouth of the passage. Inside its entrance he stood poised, ready for anything. Another moan and then silence. He edged into the darkness, straining to see. One step at a time, he felt his way. Even so, he nearly fell over the prostrate body.

Keeping his blade ready, Matthias groped with his claw-shaped left hand to identify the victim's injuries. He withdrew his hand, recognizing the stickiness and cloying scent of blood, a lot of blood. If only he could see. He must get the man to the street, where at least a little light pierced the night.

Hoping the assailants really had fled, he tucked the dagger back into his girdle and hooked his arms under the victim's armpits. With his first tug the man gasped, groaned again, and slumped as though dead. The few paces might kill the poor soul, but he surely would die if left in the alley.

Matthias inched toward the street. Panting from the exertion, at last he lowered his burden. In the dim torchlight, he searched quickly for the source of the worst bleeding. His fingers stumbled over a long gash on the forehead, still streaming. He folded his own headband into a thick square, placed it over the worst bleeding, and tied the man's headband over it, using his teeth to supplement his crippled hand.

The man's head lolled sideways, exposing his blood-streaked face to the flickering light.

Matthias stared in disbelief. "Neriah! You?" In his surprise, he relaxed his grip. Neriah's head rolled limply from his hand. Matthias knelt, motionless. Of all the people in the holy city, this man deserved no good from his hand.

"Neriah!" he called sharply. "Wake up!"

The injured man gave no response. Matthias pressed his ear to his enemy's chest. He heard nothing and couldn't even feel the rise and fall of breathing. He grabbed Neriah's shoulder and shook him. His fingers sank into limp flesh.

Matthias looked up and down the street. If the Romans saw his bloody hands and robe and the Galilean dagger in his girdle, they would arrest him, and the justice of Rome did not extend to Jewish merchants.

And if Neriah lives, Matthias thought bitterly, *he can always make things even worse for me than the Romans might.*

He pressed his fingers into Neriah's neck, searching for a heartbeat. At last he felt the large blood vessel fluttering, pulsing rapidly, weakly. There was a chance the sturdy young rabbi would survive if Matthias could get him to a physician.

Glancing around, Matthias spied a familiar landmark. Yes. Neriah's home, the house of Elul, lay just down the hill, closer than his own house, but still a formidable distance to carry anyone so weakened. It could kill him, yet there was no hope for him here.

Without further hesitation Matthias pulled the unresisting body to a sitting position. With his good hand he gripped one arm, clamped Neriah's leg in the crook of his other arm, and lurched to his feet. Once upright, he proceeded down the street, concentrating on one step at a time.

A torch smoldered in its bracket by Neriah's gate. Matthias eased the unconscious body to the pavement and banged the knocker with all his strength.

In a moment the gate cracked open. A sleepy servant peered out, raising a lantern to Matthias's face.

"I've brought your master," Matthias explained. "He's badly hurt." Only then did the gatekeeper see Neriah lying at Matthias's feet.

The man shouted for help, and in a moment servants swarmed out.

"Carefully!" Matthias warned. "Lift him carefully to that pallet. And send someone for a physician!" He was kneeling to help, when Elizabeth's horrified cry stopped him. He straightened and made way for her.

Ashen-faced, she pushed through the servants and dropped to her knees beside her stricken husband. "Neriah!" she cried brokenly, her fingers caressing his bloody face. She turned to Matthias without really seeing him. "Is he . . . ?"

"He lives, but he needs a doctor."

She looked up at the servant beside her. "Go, Samuel, get Stephen the physician. Hurry!"

"It is done, Mistress. As soon as this man told me, I sent for him." He nodded toward Matthias.

Then Elizabeth recognized him. "You! You brought him?"

"Yes."

She stood up and ordered the servants to carry Neriah into the house. Over her shoulder she said, "Please come in, Matthias. After Neriah is safe I want to talk to you."

He nodded and followed. Once inside the gate, he glanced at the gray face of the man he'd saved. "Wait!" he exclaimed. "The bandage has slipped and he bleeds afresh. Let me tighten it."

At Elizabeth's gesture the servants set down their master.

Matthias knelt and fumbled with the knot. "Here! You!" he called to the nearest servant. "Press your hand here and then help me pull the knot tight."

Blood streamed anyway.

"Press harder!" snapped Matthias. He glanced up at Elizabeth. "We need a clean, larger cloth."

She spun around, grabbed some towels from the gate room, and pressed them into Matthias's hand. He made a thick wad and the servant tied it tightly in place.

Neriah groaned. His eyes opened and stared vacantly at the circle of faces above him. His gaze came to rest at last on Matthias. Then he looked at Elizabeth. His body arched in a spasm. "Get him out of here! I won't have this swine in my home!" he cried. "Get him out . . ." He fainted again.

Elizabeth began to sob. "Take him to his room," she cried, rising to follow. To Matthias she called, "Please wait for me."

"If you wish." He watched them bear Neriah away. Left to himself, he was suddenly aware of Neriah's blood streaking his robe.

One servant lingered beside him. "I will show you where you may wait, sir," he offered.

In a small guest room near the gate, servants brought him water for cleansing, a clean garment to wear, and a flagon of warmed wine. He sipped a little and then paced the floor, wishing he could leave.

In Matthias's concern to save Neriah, he'd briefly laid aside his own animosity. Now the injured man's outburst against him had rekindled the fire of his own resentment. He tried to douse it with reasoning. After all, the man could have been out of his mind from the injury.

Nevertheless, Matthias could not forget the years of bitterness that stood between them. Their friendship had ended when they both had fallen in love with Elizabeth. When Neriah had learned that Elizabeth preferred Matthias, he had become a desperate enemy. Because of Matthias's association with boyhood friends from Nazareth who were known Zealots, Neriah went to Matthias's teachers at the School of Hillel with the false accusation that Matthias had become the leader of a Zealot band.

When in the midst of this strife, Matthias received word that his father had been accidentally killed, he rushed to Nazareth, instead of staying to defend himself. By the time he returned to Jerusalem after only a fortnight, he had been expelled from school, and Elizabeth's father, Judah ben Joed, had betrothed her to Neriah. And even though the ben Joed residence had been Matthias's home while in Jerusalem, Judah had cast him out.

Now Matthias sighed, remembering his grief. Not only had he lost Elizabeth, but she had accused him of abandoning her to Neriah. Yet he knew if he could return to that time he still would go to his suddenly bereaved family.

Matthias glanced around Neriah's and Elizabeth's guest room and wished he could go home and forget this whole accursed evening. But because of Elizabeth, he continued to wait.

At last she came, so quietly that she startled him. Worry creased her forehead. She was more beautiful, with her dusky-shadowed eyes and ebony hair, than she'd been as a girl. "The doctor is with him. He says you saved Neriah's life." A sob choked her.

For a moment he stood helpless before her weeping, and then he reached out and drew her into his arms as he had so often done with his little sisters. With her face against his chest, he smoothed her hair. "It will be all right, Elizabeth. Neriah will be all right." It was no different than when he had comforted Hannah, Sarah, Rebekah, Abigail, or Mary. He felt no stirring of desire for her.

When she finally stopped crying, he released her and told her how he'd found Neriah.

She listened, her lips still trembling. "I begged him not to go out at night without servants. He always laughs at my fears."

"Perhaps now he will be more sensible."

She looked at him skeptically. "You men! You're no different. You were out alone too."

"I've learned the ways of the streets. I'm watchful." Instinctively his hand moved to his girdle and brushed against the familiar comfort of his dagger handle.

She sighed shakily. "I doubt that anyone can be watchful enough. How can I thank you, Matthias? I owe you . . . everything."

"You owe me nothing."

"You saved him!" Her voice threatened to fail her again. "He is my life . . ."

Matthias couldn't take his eyes from her face and the look of love behind the anxiety. Yet his words came easily, naturally. "I'm glad I could help."

Impulsively she reached out and touched his hand. "We were very foolish children, weren't we? At fifteen I thought I knew my destiny . . . and I was so wrong. I never meant to hurt you. I hope you've forgiven me."

"Elizabeth, it is I who should ask for forgiveness. I am the older. I should not have sought your affection without first speaking to your father."

"Then let us agree that all is forgiven and forgotten." She smiled tenderly. "We shall be the friends we were meant to be."

"You are more like my sister," he corrected, "for your brother Reuben is truly a brother to me."

She looked at him with surprise. "After you were gone, I used to wish I was one of your sisters, for they could live with you and touch you, when I couldn't even see you."

He stood speechless, stabbed with a warning, like a soldier who has wrenched the scar of an old wound.

She continued, unaware of his inner struggle for composure. "I was childishly cruel to Neriah," she remembered. "I don't suppose I can ever make up for what I did to him when I wanted you. At first I didn't want to live. I did everything I could to anger him, but he remained patient and gentle."

She paused, casting Matthias a thoughtful look. "When our first child was born I defeated him at last. I rejected his son and cried for you. I thought he would hit me, but instead he wept and left the room.

"Later as I tended the baby, the blackness that had filled my heart for more than a year began to fade. Finally, I could see how much Neriah cared for me. He continued to love me until I could not help loving him. The more I loved him, the more I despised what I had done. I tell you this," she concluded, "so you may possibly understand the depth of my gratitude to you for rescuing him tonight."

"Elizabeth, you mustn't blame yourself," said Matthias quietly. "As you said, we were very young and foolish. But our lives have turned out well."

Her lower lip trembled again. Then she said in a rush, "I can't believe he still hates you. It must be the injury. When he's well I shall tell him how you saved his life. Surely he will forget the past and welcome you in our home."

Matthias shook his head. "Don't tell him. It doesn't matter. If you were ever to need me, I'd come. But to visit . . . Neriah may never accept me as a friend. Let it rest . . . let him rest."

"Perhaps you're right," she said and turned to leave. "I must go to him. Thank you again, Matthias, for everything."

He lifted his hand in response to her farewell gesture. "Good night, Elizabeth."

"Good night," she answered, in a voice that told him her thoughts already had fled to the bedside of her husband.

He found his way, unescorted, to the gate. The keeper let him out without a word and dropped the bar into place with a solid thud. Matthias stepped into the darkness, his hand poised near his dagger.

Seeing Elizabeth and Neriah had awakened the past, with all its pain.

Memories as vivid as yesterday flooded his mind.

He tried to push them away, to keep his attention on the night dangers of the street, but he could not.

With all the fervor of first love, he and Elizabeth had loved each other. It would be easy to be drawn into those emotions again.

When in desperation he turned his thoughts away from Elizabeth, he fell to thinking about Neriah. Neriah and Reuben had been second year students at the School of Hillel when Matthias had entered. Matthias enjoyed Reuben's gregarious nature and valued his innate honesty. And he admired Neriah's keen mind and drive for excellence in all things.

Perhaps in response to his callow admiration, Neriah had mentored Matthias during his first homesick months at the academy. Neriah patiently coached Matthias until he acquired the polished manners expected of people in the city and could speak without a thick Galilean dialect. Neriah also made it known that, by designing special tools to compensate for his crippled hand, Matthias had become a skilled blacksmith in his father's shop, and even had learned to cast bronze. Students quickly began to treat Matthias with respect.

Then at the end of Matthias's second year at the academy, because of their conflict over Elizabeth, Neriah seemed to change utterly. Wielding his power as nephew to Caiaphas, who was soon to be the High Priest, Neriah not only thwarted Matthias's future at the school, but tried to remove Matthias's best chance for supporting his family in Jerusalem. When the goldsmiths' guild rejected Matthias's application for apprenticeship, Neriah admitted he had persuaded the master goldsmith not to accept a one-handed Zealot as an apprentice, no matter how talented he might be.

Matthias could not take over his father's blacksmith shop as a life-time work, for fear the strain of hammering iron might ultimately damage the arm supporting his good hand. If Reuben had not introduced him to Shebuel, a prosperous rug merchant, he would have been hard-pressed to support his family.

As Matthias neared his own gate, the memory of young Neriah became one with the memory of the man who had raged at him tonight. Past and present merged, leaving a single image in Matthias's mind. He muttered to himself, "It wasn't the injury. Neriah does still hate me."

Two

When Matthias finally fell into his own bed that night, the dream returned.

Elizabeth stood before him, the lower part of her face concealed by a soft white veil. Her bridal attendants, carrying boughs of myrtle, their heads adorned in wreaths of fragrant blossoms, waited behind her. Sweet, beautiful Elizabeth! Her dark eyes caressed him.

He gazed back at her, also letting his look be his touch.

Suddenly her eyes narrowed. Unbelievably, searing hatred glared back at him.

"Elizabeth!" he gasped.

She laughed contemptuously. To his horror her voice had the timbre of a man's.

Matthias's mind raced. What's wrong? Oh God of our fathers! This is a man!

He grabbed the veil and ripped it off. The arrogant face of Neriah leered back at him.

Matthias lunged for him, but his hand closed on air. Neriah had retreated swiftly out of reach. When Matthias tried to follow, his legs refused to obey.

Neriah threw back his head and laughed again.

Then Matthias saw Elizabeth behind Neriah, her face pale, her eyes anguished, her hands reaching out to him until Neriah imposed himself between them.

Matthias, damp with perspiration, awoke with a jolt and sat up. For a long time he'd been free of the dream. No doubt last night's events had dredged it up from wherever dreams hide. Pulling his feet out of the tangled bed cover, he rubbed his hand across his eyes and stood up. The cool marble of the floor pressed reassuringly against his bare feet. He moved into the hall, and from a smoldering lamp he lit a smaller lamp and carried it back to his room. Bathing quickly, he said his morning prayers, and then went out into his small garden.

The eastern sky was paling. Soon the silver trumpets from the temple would sound the time of morning sacrifice. He paced around the garden. The mood evoked by the dream clung to him. He felt unclean, as if he'd touched a corpse. Reuben had suggested if he went to hear the preaching of John the Baptist, he might find release from the past. Perhaps Reuben was right.

Thumping his fist against the palm of his twisted hand, he cursed the nightmare, and as if it were a thing he could command, he said, "This is the last time! I will go to hear John."

Several weeks later, after delivering carpets to Jericho for his employer, Shebuel, Matthias sent his assistants back with the camels and set off to look for the Baptizer.

Even though Bethabara lay away from the caravan route, a sporadic stream of people plodded through the heat toward the Jordan near its outlet into the Dead Sea. Matthias joined them. Bathed in the blinding light and searing sun of the valley, he began to wonder why he'd come in midsummer.

Whatever Matthias had expected, he arrived unprepared for the sight at the river. Where the Jordan widened, a few enduring trees, filled with chirping birds, clung to the low banks. On a treeless strip of the shore, surrounded by a large crowd of people, stood a man clad in a coarse, knee-length tunic. His hair and beard tumbled onto his shoulders and chest. His eyes, accustomed to desert sun, bore the look of an eagle. Tall, muscular, and thin, he seemed like a Galilean Zealot. His resonant voice carried effortlessly across the crowd.

"Repent, for the Kingdom of Heaven is near! Prepare the way for the Lord." The man turned and waded into the river. Many people followed. One by one, John baptized them.

At the water's edge, Matthias strained to hear what the Baptizer said to each person, but he couldn't make it out. He could see, however, that the man's expression, so passionate during his speech, had softened to a captivating tenderness. Then the preacher looked toward him, and anger hardened his countenance. Matthias tensed defensively until he realized the man was glaring at someone behind him. John's voice rang out sharply: "Who warned you brood of vipers to flee the coming wrath?"

Matthias turned. A fastidious group of Pharisees were clustered just a pace away. With white-knuckled hands they tried to keep their colorful, tasseled robes from touching the dusty, sweating people on all sides.

"Don't depend on being Abraham's children. Every tree that doesn't bear good fruit will be cut down," John warned. "Even now the ax bites the roots."

The Pharisees drew their robes closer around themselves, but one called out, "What should we do to show good fruit?"

"If you have two coats, give to the one who has none," John answered. "And likewise, share your food."

Matthias admired the preacher's straightforward manner.

The Pharisees, except for one, began to move away. The almond eyes of the one, Matthias recognized. Neriah's face, heavily bearded and shaded against the sun by a light burnoose, had thinned. The wound, almost healed, slashed through his left eyebrow and disappeared under his hood, where Matthias knew it gashed a line into his hair above his ear.

Matthias raised his hand tentatively. "Good day, Neriah."

Neriah's mouth relaxed into a guarded smile. "I hear I owe you my life."

"You owe me nothing."

"I know you would have done as much for anyone," said Neriah sardonically, "but since it was me, I thank you."

Matthias bowed slightly. "I accept your thanks."

Neriah bowed and left.

The Baptist was speaking again. "I tell you, the One who comes after me is far greater than I. I am not worthy of untying his sandals." The Baptist had waded closer, and he gazed directly at Matthias. "Repent. Choose a new way of life."

His words pierced Matthias. He had almost forgotten: the kind of righteousness he'd known in his father, Aaron, and in his boyhood friend Jesus. He longed for such righteousness.

He stepped out into the water and reached for John's hand.

On his first day back in the holy city, Matthias saw Neriah again, standing with Elizabeth in a jeweler's shop. Her back was to Matthias, but Neriah's face was wholly revealed. She held up a necklace of gold and cool emerald stones. With his eyes never leaving her face, he took them and said something, and the look of tenderness and naked adoration that crossed his face stopped Matthias in his tracks.

Neriah fastened the necklace around her neck, and to Matthias's astonishment took her hand and looked as if he would kiss her in public. Laughing together, they both turned and simultaneously saw Matthias. Elizabeth called, "Oh, Matthias! How good to see you."

Neriah soberly held out his hand. "We meet again so soon."

"I left Bethabara soon after you did," said Matthias.

"Neriah told me he saw you. What did you think of John the Baptist?" asked Elizabeth.

"I think he may be a prophet," said Matthias.

Neriah pursed his lips. "Uncouth as he is, he speaks well. He has, however, angered many of my friends."

"I think we all need prophetic warnings," said Matthias, not wanting to argue, but determined to support John.

"I agree, but when he talks of the Messiah, he sounds just like another Zealot, if you will forgive my use of the term." Neriah smiled apologetically. "I mean the fanatical few, not your friends."

Matthias realized that was the nearest Neriah would ever get to an apology for his false accusation that Matthias had been a Zealot while in the School of Hillel. And for the sake of peace, he accepted it. "Well, I hope that he is correct and that the Messiah does come soon," he said.

"Yes," said Neriah. "If you will excuse me, I want to see what price I can get from the jeweler for this necklace. Good day, Matthias."

"Good day to you."

Elizabeth smiled at Neriah and then at Matthias. "God be with you, Matthias." She tucked her hand under Neriah's arm in a gesture that seemed to close out everyone else. She and Neriah seemed as devoted to one another as Matthias's sister Hannah and her husband Cleopas. To see Elizabeth so happy and to feel no remnant of desire for her was more than a relief.

As for Neriah, with him Matthias might keep an armistice, but there never could be friendship between them. So much hurt could not be assuaged with a few words and a handclasp.

Three

After a warm day's work in Shebuel's rug shop, Matthias crossed the lower city to the house of Cleopas, his brother-in-law, and his sister Hannah. Above a cheese shop run by Cleopas and his father, Ethan, the family shared six rooms.

Upon seeing Matthias at the door of the outer stairs, Cleopas exclaimed, "Come in, my wandering friend!" and embraced him with arms that could throw a bullock.

Cleopas and Elizabeth's brother Reuben claimed Matthias's affection as no friends had since the days when Jesus and Simon had shared boyhood adventures with him in Nazareth. The two Jerusalemites were as different as fire is from rock, and in spite of his unruly reddish hair, Cleopas was the rock. Now he tugged Matthias indoors and led him to the low table where Ethan sat cross-legged on a mat with Hannah and Cleopas's small sons. Ethan, a graying, weightier version of Cleopas, struggled to get up.

"Please don't rise for me, sir," begged Matthias, bowing to the elder.

Ethan settled back and smoothed his grizzled beard. His eyes, shaded by their generous brows, expressed the contentment of a heavily burdened camel that has just been granted a rest. "This once only," he conceded. "Our house is your house, Matthias."

"May your hospitality return to you fourfold, sir," Matthias answered.

The boys jumped up and ran to Matthias. "Uncle! Did you see any lions?" asked David, his green eyes alight with excitement.

"Did you see any robbers?" cried Joseph.

Matthias gathered up the boys in his arms. "No, but I saw a man in the desert, clad in garments not fit for a slave, who spoke like a prophet." Recalling his first sight of John, he said, "He looked as fierce as an eagle and spoke like an angel of the Lord."

Hannah and Tamara, a kinswoman who had mothered Cleopas and his sister Miriam after their birth mother had died, entered with a dish of fruit and a bowl of marinated vegetables. Miriam followed with bread and cheese.

Matthias lowered the boys to the floor and kissed Hannah on the cheek. "Have you prepared enough food for a guest?"

"You know we have," scolded Tamara.

As they sat to eat, Miriam asked eagerly, "Did you see John the Baptist? Do you think he really is a prophet?"

"Let Matthias speak, daughter," said Ethan. "You'll drown him with your many questions." His voice held no rebuke, and poorly concealed pride gleamed in his eyes.

Ethan dotes on his quick-minded daughter as much as if she were a son, thought Matthias with amusement. He wondered if her half-Greek mother had possessed such a passion to learn and to question. The old cheese merchant often said copper-haired Miriam was like her.

Miriam, seated opposite him, looked like a ray of light in a dark place. Matthias decided it wasn't only from her striking appearance, but also from some inner clarity and expressiveness. What a beautiful woman she would be one day.

Cleopas urged, "Tell us, Matthias. Is he a prophet?"

"He says he's the one prophesied by Isaiah, 'a voice crying in the wilderness to make way for the coming of the Lord,' and his eyes on me felt like the eyes of God. I repented and he baptized me."

The family sat quietly, their supper untouched. Cleopas spoke first, his broad face sober. "Do you think he is announcing the coming of the Messiah?"

"Come with me to hear for yourself. Everyone should hear him."

"You sound like a preacher too," Cleopas teased. "But yes, I'll go. When?"

"Tomorrow?"

Cleopas glanced at his father with raised eyebrows.

Ethan nodded.

Hannah, who had been watching the men in silence, begged, "Husband, I want to go too."

"It will be a difficult trip because of the heat in the valley, but yes, if you really wish to, come with me."

"Oh, Father. May I go to hear this man also?" asked Miriam. Her request surprised Matthias less than Hannah's, for Miriam possessed an interest in the Law more suitable to a man than a girl. Ethan, after discovering Cleopas had secretly taught her to read, was permitting her to be tutored by an elderly uncle, Rabbi Ebed.

Ethan raised his shaggy gray eyebrows, laughed, and exclaimed, "Ah. The boys and I shall have at least four days of peace." With that he said the blessing and they ate.

After supper Matthias watched Miriam with affection as she whisked by with a bundle already packed and tied. She had been a high-spirited child, but lately had displayed signs of an iron will. In the span of a breath, she could change from agreeably yielding to passionately resistant. He enjoyed her incisive mind, as always, but found her recent unpredictability unsettling. He surely wouldn't want Ethan's task of finding her a husband.

The next morning as the sun's first rays warmed the walls of the holy city, the two men, the women, and their burdened donkey ascended the long slope of the Mount of Olives. Unencumbered, the women walked ahead like two children on an outing.

What a contrast, thought Matthias. Hannah's dark hair and black eyes, and Miriam's copper hair and fair skin. His sister, in the privacy of the early hour, had thrown back her brightly embroidered hood. Miriam shaded herself, even from the morning sun, with a mantle as blue as the sky. Looking at her now, no one would guess that during childhood her nose had flaunted a generous sprinkling of freckles and usually had been in some stage of peeling.

To Matthias's surprise, the women trooped along all day with only brief rest stops. Before sunset they reached the caravansary. A wiry man, whose skin looked as brown and creased as the wilderness cliffs, took their coins and led them past a corral of donkeys. "When you have unloaded," he said, "tether your beast here. For the women's tent, I'll show you my choice ground in the courtyard."

The place he indicated was level enough, but, more important, stone walls protected two sides. With Matthias and Cleopas lying down by the other sides of the tent, the women would be secure.

While the men set up the tent, Hannah and Miriam bartered for charcoal, set it to glowing, and hung a small black pot over it. The fragrance of the lentils and leeks wafted to the men. "That smells so good!" Matthias called.

Miriam smiled as she stirred. "A bit of cumin and bay leaf spices the pot," she explained. A sooty smudge on her cheek somehow enhanced her beauty.

The jingle of camel bells and shouts of drivers announced the arrival of a caravan. Matthias swung around, took measure of the men—a group of honest merchants—and relaxed.

Twilight swiftly darkened the mountains above, but light still glowed on the wilderness east of the Jordan River. Miriam brought Matthias the hot pottage and a loaf of dry traveler's bread and knelt beside him.

"Mmm. A feast," he said.

"A poor banquet, indeed," she scoffed, but a pleased half-smile lingered on her lips as she leaned over to place the bowl in front of him.

As if seeing her clearly for the first time, Matthias couldn't take his eyes from her. Where had childhood flown? In the dim light, her face so close to his became a pale oval and her shadowed eyes, large and luminous. This little sister had become a strikingly beautiful woman. He drew back, uncomfortable at her nearness. Then, confused by his own unexpected reaction, he exclaimed awkwardly, "When you were seven, I wondered if you ever would grow up to fit your front teeth, but you surely have!"

Instead of bantering, she stood up abruptly, a pained look wiping away her smile.

Matthias scrambled to his feet. "Miriam, I was jesting, trying in my clumsy way to say you've grown very beautiful!"

She hesitated. "You truly think so?" she asked uncertainly.

"As truly as the first day follows the Sabbath. Don't you realize you are pleasing to the eye?"

"If you had been born with red hair, you wouldn't ask," she replied with a trace of her normal flippancy.

"You are all any man could want and more, Miriam."

Looking up at him soberly, she didn't answer.

"Don't go. Sit with me, please," Matthias urged.

She knelt again on his outspread cloak. He sat beside her and offered her the bread to dip into the pottage. She couldn't break it. Chuckling, he took it. "Would you starve without a strong hand to help? Here. Hold one side." With his good hand he pressed against the flat bread. It refused to crack. He raised an eyebrow. "Shall I pound it with a rock?"

Her delighted laugh put him on familiar footing with her again. He had always enjoyed her musical laughter. Now with her womanly beauty, she was a feast for both eyes and ears. She suddenly sobered. He had been staring. He shifted uneasily. She was waiting for him to speak, but he didn't know what to say.

Then he remembered the bread still in his hand and snatched at the opportunity for action. "This should do it!" he exclaimed. Pulling his brass-handled dagger from his girdle, he laid the flat loaf across the bowl and he rapped it sharply. It broke into pieces. "There you are." He gave Miriam a piece.

She took it, but her eyes were on the dagger. "I didn't know you carried such a weapon!"

"It's a keepsake, but handy on a journey."

"May I see it?"

He put the ornate hilt in her hand and watched as she turned it slowly, running her fingers along the pattern. In the fading light the brass gleamed like gold.

"A setting fine enough for jewels," she mused, "too handsome for that wicked blade. Where did you get it?"

"I made it."

"You made it!"

"Well, I made the handle. I intended it to be a decorative knife for my mother, but my father placed the longer blade of a dagger into it when he discovered I'd left it unfinished."

"I had no idea you could do anything like this." The lilt in her voice, like her laugh, touched a place deep inside him. She turned the weapon in her hand experimentally. "It does fit my hand, although the blade is long. Why didn't you finish it?"

He shrugged. "My life changed. That was the year they sent me to Jerusalem for school. Even though I had proved I could be a good ironsmith with two strong arms and one good hand, Father insisted that I become a scholar. I lost heart for finishing the knife."

"Oh," she said, her voice quiet with sympathy. She traced the twining vines and wheat once more and then handed it back. He started to take it, but stopped with his fingers curled over hers. Her hand felt very warm and small. "Miriam, I made it for a woman's hand. I'd like for you to have it," he offered on impulse.

She stared at their hands clasped together on the knife handle, and then looked up with a smile. "I will treasure it. Thank you, Matthias." Her voice seemed muffled. With a graceful motion she rose to her feet. She reminded him of a shy antelope poised for flight. Why was she leaving? He started to get up, to detain her.

Just then Cleopas sauntered over and dropped down beside him. Miriam hurried away. Matthias slumped back, disappointed.

"Is Little Sister upset?" Cleopas asked between bites.

"I don't know," Matthias answered.

Cleopas turned his full attention to his bowl. With half a mind, Matthias began to eat. When they finished and were leaning back on their elbows to watch the stars appear, Matthias asked, "Cleopas, why has Miriam not married?"

"Father spoils her, like your father did your sisters," he said with a shrug in his voice. "Several men have asked, but he won't betroth her against her wishes. If it were up to me, I'd have settled her with someone before now. Why do you ask?" He raised himself up. "Are you interested?"

The question shocked Matthias. "No! No, I just suddenly realized she's old enough." He hoped he didn't sound too abrupt, but Miriam was like a sister. He continued in a matter-of-fact tone, "Attractive as she's become, I'm surprised she wasn't promised long ago. Did you know she thinks she's not comely?"

"No. But she's too practical to worry about such things."

Matthias, appalled at such logic, wondered how Cleopas could be so blind to his own sister's vulnerability. Tonight Miriam had revealed a fragile side of her nature that her brother should have noticed long ago.

The next day passed quickly. Matthias walked with Miriam, while Hannah strode beside Cleopas and the donkey. At rest stops Matthias played the small harp he carried in his pack, and Cleopas sang. The women idled in whatever small shade they found and sometimes sang along.

That night in the caravansary at Jericho, Matthias helped Miriam start her cooking fire. He set the stones in place to hold the pot, and then leaned back on his heels to fan the coals. "I'm glad you came with us," he said. "You and Hannah have made this journey seem like a festival."

She glanced up from the already bubbling pot of lamb and vegetables they'd purchased. "I love the wilderness. When I sleep in a tent, it reminds me of the Feast of Booths. I envy desert people, who still live like our Father Abraham."

Later, stretched on the ground beside the women's tent, Matthias thought Abraham's Sarah must have been like Miriam—strong and very desirable.

The following day when they reached Bethabara, John was speaking as stirringly as Matthias had remembered. His words—wise, righteous, and direct—rekindled Matthias's hope that the preacher was preparing Israel for the coming of the Messiah. Finally, the Baptist cried, "Repent and be baptized!" And as before, scores of people followed him into the river. Among the first were Cleopas and Hannah. Miriam stood beside Matthias for a moment with her head bowed. Then she too waded into the water, her dress swirling around her with each step.

After baptizing all the penitents, John stepped out of the water and stood quietly. Although it was obvious he had finished preaching for the day, people lingered around him, loathe to leave. Suddenly the Baptist looked up, westward, and raised his hand in a salute.

"Look!" he exclaimed. "The Lamb of God comes! He is the One I told you about, who will baptize you with the Holy Spirit. He is the Son of God!"

Matthias's heart leaped with excitement.

In the direction John gestured, Matthias saw a man standing alone on an embankment at the edge of the throng. He seemed to tower in silhouette against the afternoon sky, his features undiscernible.

People turned and muttered, "Who? Which one does he mean?"

But Matthias knew. He had seen. As he elbowed his way toward the stranger, the man descended and approached John. Closer up, surprisingly, he was no taller than John. When Matthias drew near to the two men, the one John had called the Lamb of God threw back his mantle, exposing coppery, sun-bleached hair, and turned toward Matthias. A smile of recognition lighted his sunburned face.

"Matthias!" he exclaimed.

Matthias gaped. "Jesus! Jesus, is it you?" He grabbed the outstretched hand. "Are you the Promised One?"

Four

Jesus gripped Matthias's hand with the strength of an ironsmith.

"Are you the One John spoke of? Are you the Promised One?" Matthias repeated. His racing heart robbed him of breath.

Jesus smiled, his teeth flashing white behind his heavy beard. He said, "John speaks of the Messiah."

Matthias couldn't take his eyes from the bronzed face of his friend. Unaccountably, he wanted to retreat from Jesus' intense gaze, but the powerful handclasp held him close. His discomfort must have shown, for Jesus sobered and released him. In some indefinable way his friend seemed like a stranger. True, they hadn't met for many months, not even for Passover, but . . .

Matthias stammered, "I thought . . . John pointed at you!"

Jesus glanced at the Baptist and then said to Matthias, "You find me changed." Quietly, as though to himself, he added, "I've walked a long way these past forty days in the wilderness. I'm not the man you knew." He drew a breath and let it out slowly. "And yet . . . I am!" Undisguised joy softened the weathered lines around his eyes, but he offered no explanation. Power and authority emanated from him. In his dusty, travel-stained homespun, he stood like a king. No wonder he had seemed so tall at first glance. "I must return to Galilee," he said. "And you, I suppose, to Jerusalem. May the Father watch over you, Matthias."

Before Matthias could gather his wits to ask more, Jesus turned, spoke briefly to John, and then threaded his way through the crowd.

Matthias was still transfixed by Jesus when Cleopas touched his arm. "Who was that man?" he asked.

"What? Oh . . . an old friend from Nazareth." Matthias couldn't find words for the emotions and questions Jesus had evoked.

On their return trip up the narrow zigzagging road to Jerusalem, Matthias and Cleopas took turns urging the donkey. After the first elation of baptism, the women walked as though dreaming. Cleopas too soon fell into a reverie. Trudging upward, surrounded by stark slopes of tumbled brown rock, Matthias wondered what Jesus had meant about being in the wilderness for forty days. *Surely not here. Nothing lives here,* he thought.

Miriam climbed tirelessly beside Matthias. Although she matched his remoteness with a solitude of her own, the fact that she was a woman and, as such, had to be cared for, nagged at his attention. At least she was undemanding. Matthias made no effort to converse; he couldn't get his mind off Jesus. Irrational as it seemed, he wished he could have followed his friend back to Galilee.

When Cleopas called a halt, the four of them collapsed under the shelter of an overhanging rock.

Cleopas remarked, "You've been very quiet since you spoke to your friend. Did he bear bad news?"

Matthias pulled off his headband to let the thirsty air dry his damp hair, and he mopped his forehead. "Seeing Jesus brought back a lot of memories. After my hand was crushed, the other boys had no time for me, but Jesus became my friend. Soon Simon joined him as my friend. We were an unlikely trio—a crippled boy, the son of a Zealot, and Jesus—but we became inseparable, helping each other with chores and as we grew older, roaming the mountains together. Jesus soothed Simon's anger over the crucifixion of his uncle, and he somehow inspired me to try the impossible. He showed me how to do as much with one hand as I'd done with two. Then when Father was killed by that runaway chariot, Jesus made me believe I could, at eighteen, care for my family as well as a man."

"I didn't see Jesus!" Hannah exclaimed with surprise.

"You probably wouldn't have recognized him," said Matthias.

"How has he changed?" asked Hannah.

"It's difficult to explain," said Matthias. "He just seems . . . different."

Miriam exclaimed, "You used to tell me about your friend Jesus. I still think about some of his sayings."

"Ah, yes! But you were so little. I'm surprised you understood any of them."

Her slow smile stirred in him a desire to touch the curve of her cheek, as a sculptor would, to memorize it. How could he have thought her still a child? Her eyes captured light from the sun-drenched cliffs and glinted green as the waves of the Great Sea. Engrossed with her comeliness, he almost missed her terse remark.

"I didn't say I understood. I only said I remembered."

Matthias threw back his head and laughed. She debated like a man. He felt like clapping her on the back for a point well made. What a contradiction she was!

"I can't say I understood either," he admitted, "although I tried. I haven't seen him for a long time."

Miriam remarked, "But you will see more of him now."

Her invasion into his unspoken thoughts jolted him. "Why do you say that?"

"Your face has a look when you speak of him . . . the way you used to look," she answered enigmatically.

Cleopas and Hannah stared at him questioningly. Matthias shrugged. Women truly were a mystery. To Cleopas he said, "Shouldn't we be moving on? I hear the bells of a caravan. We don't want to walk in its dust and droppings."

Refreshed from the brief rest, they returned to the road. While the others talked about John the Baptist, Matthias puzzled about Jesus again. What had happened to him? Could he be the One about whom John was preaching? If so, why did he not admit it? Suddenly Matthias remembered that silence could communicate as well as words. Jesus had not denied it either.

With little argument Matthias obtained Shebuel's consent to go to Galilee and also received a fatherly warning against the danger of getting involved with false messiahs and Zealots.

Matthias lingered for a fortnight with the seven men who stayed close to Jesus. All were Galilean—Andrew and his brother Peter, Philip, Nathanael, John, who had barely begun to grow a beard, James—John's brother—and Simon, Matthias's boyhood friend, whom the others called the Zealot. They were a rugged lot. If Shebuel could see them, he might consider them all Zealots.

Simon, eager-eyed as a young fox, said several times it was like old times to be with Matthias and Jesus again. To Matthias it was not anything like old times. In their youth Jesus had asked the same questions he and Simon had asked, but always had found different answers. Now Jesus didn't even ask the same questions, and his answers probed the deepest recesses of their minds and hearts. Matthias listened intently and weighed what he heard against all he had ever learned. His friend, a worker of woods, had become an incomparable teacher without benefit of the School of Hillel.

Even though, according to Simon, Jesus had turned water to wine at a wedding, Matthias could not bring himself to ask again the question Jesus had evaded at Bethabara. He went home uncertain. Could Jesus be the Messiah?

Once Matthias was back in the holy city, the early rains began and winter's chill settled over the land. Restless to rejoin Jesus, he chafed under his obligation to his elderly employer. In some ways Shebuel had become like a father to him. The old man relied on Matthias to oversee all business whenever he felt too infirm to walk down the hill to the shop.

The cold season clung to the mountains of Judea. Days dragged by, week following drab week. After being with Jesus, Matthias's duties as Shebuel's steward seemed purposeless. Only the evenings spent with Cleopas, Hannah, and especially Miriam eased Matthias's frustration. Miriam listened avidly to his discussions with Cleopas and occasionally posed questions that neither man could answer. And she grew more beautiful.

At last the north wind ceased and the first pale pink clouds of almond blossoms began to grace brown slopes. Matthias longed to visit Jesus and the green mountains of Galilee, but Shebuel sent him south to Alexandria. When he returned he barely had time to complete his purification—the prescribed bathings and avoidance of unclean contacts before Passover—but at last he would see Jesus. At the beginning of the Holy Week, he waited eagerly for some word from either Jesus or Simon.

Instead of them, Reuben, robed in one of the dark red fabrics from his own dye shop, appeared at the rug shop entrance just as Matthias was securing the street door for the night. Although his smooth black hair and beard were as flawlessly groomed as ever, he looked somehow disheveled. He said anxiously, "A man named Jesus is in trouble. I'm sure he's your friend—the one I met when your father died." With an uneasy glance over his shoulder, he stepped inside and gestured for Matthias to close the door.

Matthias obeyed and barred it. "What about Jesus?"

"You must warn him of his danger! He's sowing seeds to reap a whirlwind! He drove the high priest's money changers out of the temple! Not only that, Neriah says when Caiaphas's men confronted him, he told them he could destroy the temple and rebuild it in three days!"

Matthias shook his head, bewildered. "That doesn't sound like Jesus."

"Neriah witnessed it all," Reuben said firmly, "and he's reporting to the high priest right now. He says if the Nazarene appears in the temple again, guards will seize him."

"This has to be a misunderstanding."

"No. Jesus has challenged our rulers—our own people in our temple."

"Reuben, they aren't my people or yours. You know those money changers are worse thieves than the publicans. They exact profits from poor country folk who can barely scrape together an offering. And Caiaphas skims his portion from the top of the money changers' profits."

Reuben didn't argue. "I hoped I could persuade you to stay away from your Nazarene friend. He's creating dangerous enemies."

"I'll warn him."

"You won't take heed for your own safety?"

"No."

Reuben huffed in irritation, "I guess I knew you wouldn't listen. I must go. I don't want Neriah to guess I came here."

"So Neriah is up to his old tricks."

"It's nothing personal against you. He doesn't remember Jesus is your friend."

"I won't keep it a secret, but it's best that you stay out of it." He led Reuben between piles of carpets to a door that opened onto a narrow back alley.

Reuben's lean face was etched with worry. "Please get Jesus to leave the city. He may be building a fire that could consume you."

"I'll tell him what you said, and I'm grateful for your concern, but Jesus is not a political agitator. As soon as I can find out what really happened, I'll talk to Neriah. If he understands, he may be able to help."

"I don't know. Jesus has enraged him and will have angered Caiaphas, who is second only to God as far as Neriah is concerned."

Matthias searched for Jesus, but among the thousands of Passover pilgrims he saw no familiar Galilean faces. That night he crossed the upper city to see Neriah anyway. When he arrived the household was quiet. Apparently Elizabeth and the children had retired, but Neriah welcomed him and showed him to a comfortable garden seat.

After courteous greetings the two sat momentarily silent. Then both started to speak at the same time.

Neriah laughed. "You first!"

"I was about to say the same, but all right. I came to ask if you might help a friend of mine who is in trouble."

"What kind of trouble?"

"He has upset the temple authorities, I'm afraid."

Neriah leaned forward, a troubled look on his face. "You speak of the Nazarene preacher?"

"Yes. You see, he's not a political troublemaker. I realize what he did was . . . disturbing . . . but he is a righteous man, who only teaches and preaches."

"Perhaps you haven't heard him recently. Today he sounded like he wanted to destroy what we hold most sacred." Neriah stood up and began to pace nervously while he talked. "I'm afraid I can't help your friend, but you can. Persuade him to depart from the city and to leave teaching to educated rabbis."

Matthias rose, furious that once again Neriah was standing against him. Through tight lips he said, "I'm sorry to have bothered you."

Neriah gripped his hand and arm. "Matthias, I'm sorry. Believe me, if it was anything else, I'd do what I could."

"Yes. Well, I won't keep you."

Surprisingly, Neriah accompanied him to the gate, trying to make amends. So Matthias dampered his anger and tried to reciprocate. As he started down the street, Neriah called, "Matthias, I hope you won't be getting involved with the Nazarene. Men like him all end up the same way."

"I'm already involved. He's my friend."

The day after Passover Matthias found Jesus on Solomon's Porch, carrying on a dialogue with a small group of learned men. While Matthias waited at the edge of the gathering, Simon, in an excited whisper, described how Jesus had thrown over the money changers' tables. "You should have seen him, Matthias. Judas the Gaulenite could not have done it better."

When Matthias was ten, the Gaulenite had directed a rebellion against Rome, which had led most of the men of Sepphoris to crucifixion. Simon's uncle had perished on one of the two thousand crosses that had lined the road between Sepphoris and Nazareth. Suppressing a shudder, Matthias whispered, "Did Jesus threaten to destroy the temple?"

"No. He said if the rulers destroyed it, he could rebuild it in three days."

Matthias considered this information. "Did he really mean . . . why would they . . . how could he . . . ?" he faltered.

Simon smiled indulgently. His voice rose to an undertone. "What does it matter? The important thing is, he can do anything he says he can." His eager eyes turned toward Jesus, who now stood a few paces away conversing with an elderly Jew. "Come," he murmured. "Stay close to him. Don't miss a word."

Needing no invitation, Matthias followed Jesus everywhere. Spellbound, he forgot about Reuben's warning. Like other rabbis at Passover, Jesus taught throughout the marble courts of the temple. Jews from Alexandria, Cappadocia, Babylon, and Rome paused, and then stayed to hear him. Even temple guards joined his growing audience.

That night Matthias went with Jesus and his closest friends to the home of Josiah the weaver and his wife. Their home was above Josiah's shop. Late in the evening, a knock rattled the outer door. Josiah's wife admitted a man robed in the coarse brown cloth of a servant and led him to Jesus. When the visitor threw back his hood, the faltering lamplight revealed Nicodemus, one of the wealthiest members of the Sanhedrin, the supreme council and tribunal of the Jews. The Sanhedrin had civil, criminal, and religious jurisdiction.

Nicodemus did not mince words. "Rabbi, we know you are a teacher from God. You couldn't do the things you do unless God was with you."

Jesus beckoned him to a seat in the midst of the humbly clad working people. Dropping to a stool in front of Nicodemus, he extended his hand palm up toward the new guest, as if offering him a gift. "I bring you the truth. A man must be born anew to see the Kingdom of God."

Bewildered, Nicodemus exclaimed, "Can a man enter his mother's womb a second time and be born again?"

In an urgent tone Jesus answered, "Don't be astonished when I say you must be born once more. Like the invisible wind, a birth comes. You neither know where new life comes from, nor where it shall go. Spiritual birth is that way too."

Nicodemus asked, "But . . . how can all this be?"

Matthias detected a quiver of longing in the Pharisee's voice. Or were his own desires coloring his judgment? *What would it be like,* Matthias wondered, *if I could start over.* He tried to picture himself as he'd once dreamed—an artisan of gold. A second chance couldn't give him a whole hand, nor erase the pain of betrayal and grief. *I need to be reborn, like Jesus says . . . but it's impossible. What does he mean?*

Suddenly Jesus stood up. In frustration, Matthias realized his thoughts had distracted him from the brief discourse.

Nicodemus pushed himself to his feet, his expression showing he was a man out of his depth. "Rabbi . . . I thank you," he said haltingly. At the door he paused to draw his hood around his face and then left.

A young man beside Matthias remarked, "The teacher mystifies the learned men of Jerusalem and commands the respect of the wealthiest."

"You know Nicodemus?" Matthias asked.

"Only by sight. A friend of mine, also wealthy, has had business with him. Nicodemus commands respect wherever he goes. His friendship is worth cultivating."

The speaker's eyes gleamed with the passion of a Galilean, but his speech identified him as Judean, a prosperous Judean by the look of his finely woven robe and his fastidiously groomed beard.

Curious, Matthias asked, "Are you a disciple of the Nazarene?"

The short, stocky man smiled, lowered his voice, and answered, "I believe I am." He nodded toward their host and chuckled. "I stayed home tonight just to appease my Uncle Josiah. Now I'm glad, although I hate to let Uncle know he's right." He grinned boyishly.

"Will you go with Jesus when he leaves the city?" Matthias asked, wishing he himself could go.

"Yes. I will."

Matthias could tell the man had decided even as he spoke. He liked the weaver's young nephew, whose lively face and quick temperament reminded him of both Reuben and Simon. "Perhaps we'll meet again, then," said Matthias. "Matthias bar Aaron."

The man gripped his hand firmly. "An honor to meet a fellow Judean. I'm Judas . . . of Kerioth . . . Judas Iscariot."

Matthias did not correct Iscariot's assumption that he was Judean. He'd made a common mistake which pleased Matthias. In order to avoid discrimination, Matthias had worked intensively to conquer his Galilean dialect.

When Judas excused himself, Matthias went to Jesus and said, "The Pharisees are saying you want to destroy the temple. And when you overturned the tables of the money changers, you antagonized Caiaphas. My friend Reuben says you're in danger. Perhaps that rich man came to spy on you."

Jesus shook his head. "Nicodemus poses no threat, but thank you for your concern." As though in afterthought, he added, "I will leave the city when the feast ends, not from fear, but because I must preach about the Kingdom of God throughout Judea."

Matthias exclaimed, "How I wish I could come with you!"

Simon appeared at Jesus' side, his curly hair and beard surrounding his wide smile like a halo. He exclaimed, "You should be with us!"

Jesus, however, neither invited nor forbade.

"Unfortunately, I'm not free to choose," said Matthias. "Mother and Grandmother need my steward's pay. For that matter, Shebuel is almost as dependent on me as Mother and Grandmother."

"You are choosing," Jesus corrected. "But remember your vow to trust God, and you will find what you seek."

"Yes," said Matthias. How well he remembered. He and Jesus and Simon had climbed the mountain above Nazareth after visiting the fresh tomb of Matthias's father. Jesus had eased Matthias's grief by helping him to see God's love, in spite of his loss. With inexpressible longing, Matthias had made a vow to learn to trust God as much as Jesus did.

Now he quietly renewed that vow.

By the end of the evening Matthias was bursting with the flood of his own questions. When he reached his home in the upper city, he snuffed the lamps in his room and sat on his Roman-style couch. He glanced around the moonlit spacious sleeping quarters, which were only a tenth of the house. He'd come a long way from being the poor Galilean cripple. *All this was as important as my very life when I purchased it, and now it means absolutely nothing.*

His baptism had renewed in him a longing for God he had not experienced since boyhood. Could he know God in the way Jesus seemed to suggest? He might, if he could be with Jesus daily. *Surely my soul will shrivel like my hand if I do not follow Jesus. But what can I do?* Wearily he stretched out on his bed.

At dawn he awoke with the shape of a plan. He considered it, welcomed it, and dismissed all thought of Reuben's anxious warning.

Five

With an urgency born of his desire for a new life, Matthias resigned from his position with Shebuel, sold his house and possessions, and trained another of Shebuel's men, Tobias, to take his place. By the time he had accomplished this, King Herod had thrown John the Baptist into prison, and Jewish rulers were arguing vehemently against Jesus.

This only made Matthias more eager to join his friend in Galilee. He quickly settled his affairs and took money to his mother and grandmother in Emmaus, leaving a larger portion in safekeeping for them with Shebuel. Joel, his personal servant, whom he'd freed from slavery, would live with Shebuel, but not as a servant. Matthias believed, and Shebuel agreed, that the young man should receive an education worthy of his talent.

Although Joel was only eleven years younger than Matthias, he was like a son. Matthias had been enraged by the boy's hurts—starvation and beatings—before Shebuel had purchased him for Matthias. Then Joel's eagerness to help his one-handed master had won Matthias's heart.

So early on Matthias's last morning in Jerusalem, he took the young freedman to the School of Hillel. When they reached the tall facade Matthias said, "In all Jerusalem no man is more just than Rabbi Joash. If anyone can grant you an opportunity, he will."

Joel, attired in a white tunic similar to a student's simple garb, followed him up the broad steps to the colonnaded entry.

Matthias continued, "Rabbi Joash advised me, chastened me, and forgave my foolishness. If it had been his decision, I'd be a rabbi today."

Twelve years had passed since Matthias had been expelled from the academy. He ought to have stayed and defended himself against Neriah's accusations. He'd been driven by anger at Neriah, almost as much as by grief. Now he prayed Joel would have the opportunity he had forfeited so rebelliously.

Joel met his glance and smiled, transforming his thin, sparsely bearded face from plainness to what the Greeks would call beauty. His brown eyes flashed with quick intelligence.

"Hold your head high," Matthias reminded. "Whatever your beginnings, you're a Jew now. And your mental gifts mark you as a scholar." He waved aside Joel's help with the door and gripped the handle with his good hand. Inside, the unforgettable smell of ancient cedar, parchments, and ink wafted him back to his school days. He strode to a familiar door and knocked.

"Enter!" called a muffled voice.

Matthias swung the door open, stepped over the threshold, and froze. Instead of silver-haired Joash, Neriah sat at the rabbi's table.

The Pharisee stared. He found his tongue first. "Matthias! What do you want here?"

"I came to see Rabbi Joash."

"He is ill. Last winter a seizure robbed him of speech for a while. Now he no longer teaches."

"What a tragedy!" gasped Matthias. "I'm so sorry. I didn't know."

Neriah looked uncomfortable. They both knew he was the reason Matthias had maintained no direct contact with the school. "Is there anything I can do for you? I'm trying to fill Rabbi Joash's position."

Matthias dreaded having to trust Joel to this man; the recent goodwill between them had not yet been proven. To go over Neriah's head, however, surely would break their fragile peace. Carefully Matthias introduced Joel. "God has gifted this young man with the heart and mind of a scholar. He wishes to enter the academy."

Neriah smiled at Joel. "Then let him speak for himself. From what tribe do you come, Joel?"

"I can't remember my parents, sir."

"Then you are not a Jew by birth?"

"I don't know, sir. I was seven when my Lord Shebuel purchased me in Damascus and brought me to serve Matthias. Now that I am free, I want to serve God as a scribe or rabbi."

"Who taught you about the One True God?"

"Matthias bar Aaron, sir."

Neriah turned to Matthias. "No synagogue school?"

"No, but Rabbi Hasrah, in the lower city, has taught him daily for the past two years."

"Rabbi Hasrah. I've never heard of him."

"He returned three years ago from the great synagogue of Alexandria, desiring to finish his days in the holy city. He chose Joel to be his last student."

"An Alexandrian Jew."

"Yes, but a Pharisee of Pharisees!"

Neriah arose from his chair and began to pace the floor as he talked. "Matthias, remember the disagreements in this academy between the Babylonian Jews and the Alexandrian Jews? And two years of instruction can scarcely make up for seven or eight years in a synagogue school."

"But surely they would examine him and base their decision on his knowledge and ability."

"If Joel is extremely gifted, they might accept him."

"He truly is."

Neriah looked sincerely relieved. He took Joel's hand. "I'll present your case. Where may I send you a message?"

"To the house of Shebuel ben Azariah, sir. And thank you, sir." Joel beamed with happy relief.

Neriah nodded affably and said, "Matthias, tomorrow night Reuben and his father are dining with me. Will you join us?"

"Thank you, but I'm leaving in the morning for Galilee."

"Ah, then when you come back perhaps we can celebrate your return. Elizabeth would like that."

"I won't be coming back . . . to live. I've sold everything and I'm going to become a disciple of Jesus."

Neriah winced as if he'd been slapped. Sparks of anger flashed in his dark eyes. "The Nazarene!" he sputtered. "But surely you can't mean . . . You must know . . ."

"I have listened to him, and I believe he speaks the truth."

"And does Joel also listen to the Nazarene?" Neriah asked sharply.

"No. Joel doesn't know him."

Neriah returned to his table, leaned his hands on it, and bowed his head. Without looking up, he said, "I cannot imagine selling everything to follow that . . . Zealot agitator. If word of your folly gets out, you must not expect me to work a miracle for Joel."

Matthias stepped to the table and waited for Neriah to look up. "But you will try, for Joel's sake," Matthias urged quietly.

With tight lips and a sigh, he said, "I'll try."

They parted with cautious courtesy. As Matthias followed Joel through the door, Neriah called, "Matthias!"

They stared at each other. The Pharisee shook his head slowly and said, "Never mind."

Outside Matthias stamped down the street, as angry as he'd ever been at the nephew of Caiaphas. He'd been simpleminded to think they might be friends again. Nevertheless he said, "Joel, when the rabbis question you, they will admit you. Our Law commands this justice."

The next day, with a small traveling bag slung over his shoulder, Matthias went to the house above the cheese shop before leaving the city. The women were alone. They dropped their mending at the sight of him. Hannah ran to him and said anxiously, "Brother, I can't believe you're doing this."

Matthias put a fatherly arm around her. "Hannah, only good will come of whatever Jesus does."

"I pray you're right." She pulled away from him. "Let me pack some of our dried figs and cheese for your journey. Keep him here, Miriam," she called over her shoulder.

Miriam, unnaturally quiet until now, asked, "How can you be sure of good? You admitted you scarcely knew Jesus anymore."

"It's true he sometimes seems like a stranger. But in spite of that if you knew him as I do, I think you would want to follow him too."

She searched his face with eyes as dark as the darkest green chalcedony. "I think not," she answered firmly. "Rabbi Ebed says he has the power to stir people to rebellion."

Her reaction startled him. Suddenly he cared very much about having her agree with him. "I respect your teacher, but he doesn't know Jesus."

"He watched him throughout Passover. He says people follow the Nazarene like sheep, and that is dangerous. Oh, Matthias, why did you give up every-thing you've worked for, for this man who could lead you to . . ." Her voice broke. Tears sprang to her eyes and spilled over.

"Miriam," he murmured, "don't cry!" Placing his hands on her shoulders, he drew her close and whispered, "Please don't cry."

She melted against him, quiet and trusting.

Since they had walked together on the Jericho Road, he had delighted more and more in her presence, but had thought his feeling was brotherly affection.

With a shock, he realized he loved her with the love of a man for a woman. Embracing her for the briefest moment, he willed his body to remember the feel of her, and then held her at arm's length. "I love you too much to be able to leave you in tears," he said. "Please wish me well."

"Oh, Matthias. I've always loved you more than anyone else. I'm so afraid for you . . ."

At the sound of Hannah returning, Matthias let go of Miriam.

His sister placed a tightly wrapped pouch in his hand. "Send us word as soon as you can," she urged, unaware she had interrupted anything more than the usual farewell.

Distractedly Matthias answered, "Yes . . . yes, of course."

Miriam surreptitiously dashed the tears from her eyes while Hannah preceded them down the stairs.

In the shop Cleopas caught Matthias in a rough embrace. "Go with God, my brother. I'm glad if you've found what you were seeking."

"I have. I look forward to the day when you all know Jesus as I do." Parting was more difficult than Matthias had anticipated. He gripped Cleopas's hand one last time, stooped to kiss Hannah, and considered kissing Miriam's cheek too, but stopped at the quickening of his pulse. She was no longer a sister to him.

"You won't forget us, will you?" she asked, meeting his eyes in her disconcertingly direct way.

"You know I won't," he answered. But as he said it, he came to himself. In order to become a disciple he had cast aside the responsibilities of family and home. His blossoming love for Miriam could not be allowed to come to fruition. He was wronging her if he led her to desire him. As lightly as he could, he said, "Perhaps you'll be wed by the time I return." From her reaction he knew his words had accomplished his purpose.

The hurt that had sprung into Miriam's eyes haunted him all the way to Galilee, but he told himself it was for the best, because he had nothing to offer her. By the time he reached Capernaum, he had convinced himself he'd done right. By now Miriam would have forgotten his impulsive declaration of love.

From Capernaum Matthias climbed up into the mountains of Galilee to search for Jesus. Everywhere people were talking about him. Men in fields, women on their doorsteps, travelers at the wells, merchants with heavy-laden carts, and scholarly rabbis—all had heard of him. They said he was great, like John the Baptist. More than that—in Cana he had healed the dying son of the ruler. And now, they said, he had returned to Nazareth.

The second day from Capernaum, Matthias walked rapidly, ignoring the increasing heat of the day. While gritty dust sifted over his sandaled feet, he pondered over all he had heard. Jesus was doing things not seen since the days of the prophets. First wine from water, now a miraculous healing. Such power could come only from God. Matthias's heart began to pound with more than the exertion of crossing the high valley in the heat of the afternoon.

A cloud of dust approached from the west. At its forefront Matthias discerned mounted men under the banner of Rome. As they neared, he left the road to give them the right of way. A full legion marched past, sweat dripping from their faces, muscular arms glistening. The squinting eyes of those nearest flicked over Matthias with distaste. Then they passed on in disciplined order.

Matthias stared at their retreating backs. For so long Israel had been under the heel of the Gentiles. And for generations they had waited for the Messiah to free them forever from oppression. Without the Messiah, all the swords in Israel would not prevail against Rome. Yet with the Promised One, even Rome would submit to the Kingdom of God.

Could Jesus be the One—the Messiah?

At the point where the road branched toward Sepphoris Matthias left it and followed his memory up the north slope of the mountain that cradled Nazareth. Near the top he paused, wiped the sweat from his face, and looked back. Cana was now a white splotch on the far side of the valley. Sepphoris lay hidden behind the hills to the west. The fertile plain between them was dotted with fields and smaller villages, some just clusters of houses, clinging like white beads to the brown thread of the caravan route.

He and Jesus and Simon had watched the caravans from this mountain. He had felt that the world was at his feet. He'd wanted to be an artisan in gold, to create works for the temple itself, while Simon could think only of fighting, like his Zealot uncles. And Jesus—he'd never dreamed with them.

The fingers of night were beginning to weave a dark cloak for the quiet streets when Matthias reached the home of Joseph. After a brief reunion with Jesus, he lodged with Simon.

In the morning they arose early, prepared themselves, and went to the synagogue, where they met Jesus and several other disciples. They entered as a group and sat together near the elevated teacher's platform in the center of the large room.

When the ruler of the synagogue invited Jesus to read the Scriptures he stood and read eloquently, " 'The Spirit of the Lord is on me, because he has anointed me to preach good news to the poor. He has sent me to proclaim freedom for the prisoners and sight for the blind, to release the oppressed, to proclaim the year of the Lord's favor.' " The dry rasp of the parchment seemed to echo in the quiet room as he carefully rolled the scroll and handed it back to the attendant.

Many rabbis said that Scripture from Isaiah referred to the Messiah, and the way Jesus had read it made it seem like he was reading about himself.

If he says he is the Messiah, I'll believe it without a doubt, thought Matthias.

But Jesus refused to comment. Rejecting the teacher's seat, he sat again with his disciples. Matthias felt the weight of everyone's stare. He could imagine what they were thinking. They invited teachers to read, expecting them to preach. No doubt Jesus' reputation from Judea and the rest of Galilee had reached their ears and they expected him to do even more for his hometown.

Without standing, Jesus turned and simply said, "Today, in your presence, Isaiah's prophecy is being fulfilled."

The Nazarenes looked at one another, frowning but uncertain, thrown off guard by his unexpected behavior. Matthias squirmed under the growing tension. He wondered why Jesus was rejecting the honor of preaching. The graciousness of his reading could scarcely reduce the insult of his refusal to teach.

A man in the congregation, seething with quick Galilean anger, shattered the silence. "Isn't this Joseph's son, whom we have known from infancy? Who does he think he is?"

The room rumbled with questions. Jesus didn't move or say a word while the Nazarenes committed themselves to their anger. Matthias watched, puzzled and uncomfortable. The other disciples looked more expectant than worried, but it was not their hometown.

Finally in a voice that carried effortlessly above the muddle, Jesus called, "You are thinking, 'Physician, heal yourself. Demonstrate your power in your hometown first. Show us more than you showed Capernaum.' " He paused.

The congregation quieted, but someone muttered, "Who is this son of a carpenter, to tell us what we think?"

Without moving, Jesus said, "You are proving the truth that no prophet is received with favor in his hometown. I must remind you that although Israel had many widows, God sent Elijah to one in Sidon, and although Israel had many lepers, God sent a Syrian to Elisha to be cleansed."

On all sides men leaped to their feet and began to berate him openly. "Who do you think you are? Elijah or Elisha?"

"Does he make us less than Gentile dogs?"

"Cast him out!" a harsh voice shouted.

Matthias's spine prickled at the unleashed hatred facing them. He and Simon jumped up to shield Jesus, but hands grabbed them from all sides, dragging them away.

Enraged men drove Jesus from the building and up the street. They shoved and slapped their captive, pushing him before them. The road they climbed ended at a well-known cliff, a sheer drop at the edge of town.

Matthias grappled with the writhing mass of bodies between him and Jesus. His throat burned from shouting, but he couldn't hear himself.

The memory of everyone's fears for Jesus' safety assailed him. Jesus must live!

And at this impossible moment, his love for Miriam could not be denied. He too must live, to see her again.

He fought desperately against the mob.

Six

Now, more than any time in his life, Matthias felt the handicap of his deformed left hand. Searing pain shot to his elbow as contracted tendons, fused to bone, screamed. He reeled, dizzy and nauseated. Then the clamor began to fade. The hands let go. His pain peaked and eased back to a throbbing ache. Willing the gray cloud in his head to go away, Matthias peered at the men around him. They stood frozen. Matthias followed their gaze and saw Jesus, free and facing them, at the edge of the precipice.

In the abrupt quiet, an eagle screeched and a nervous sheep bleated somewhere below. Like that day at the Jordan River, Jesus suddenly seemed head and shoulders taller than those surrounding him. He lifted his arms, as if in benediction. When he stepped forward, men backed away. Without a word, he walked through them, parting them like Moses had parted the sea.

The disciples separated themselves from the Nazarenes and hurried after their teacher, glancing back from time to time like a protective rear guard.

Jesus strode along unruffled and apparently unsurprised by the riot, but Matthias was shaken. How could old neighbors think of killing Jesus? More had happened than he could understand.

When they reached Capernaum, Matthias lodged with the fisherman Andrew in his house under the lakeshore trees. Crowds gathered daily by the shore to hear Jesus teach. Never had a person spoken like him. He didn't refer to any of the great rabbis, and his wisdom surpassed theirs. Matthias noticed others doing as he did—committing precepts to memory in the manner they had learned in synagogue school as children. Whenever Jesus paused their lips moved silently as they repeated to themselves all he had said.

On the Sabbath after their return to Capernaum, Jesus healed a demon-possessed man in the synagogue. Afterward, as the disciples followed Jesus to Peter's house, Simon said, "The whole countryside will hear of this by tomorrow. People from miles around will come to him."

"Yesterday beside the sea, it looked like the whole countryside already had come," said Matthias.

Judas Iscariot, who had been with Jesus since Passover, exclaimed, "At this rate, he soon will have all Israel at his feet!"

Simon's black eyes gleamed. "And then Rome!"

"Spoken like a true Zealot." Matthias laughed, but the thought excited him.

When they reached the fisherman's home Jesus healed Peter's mother-in-law of a fever illness. Casting out the demon had dramatized Jesus' power, but this gentle healing brought a lump to Matthias's throat.

At sunset, with the Sabbath ended, people began to arrive in twos, threes, and whole families. Jesus walked among them, touching, blessing, and healing them. Moved beyond words, Matthias followed him from one person to another, watching him heal people with all manner of diseases, as well as the deaf, the mute, the blind, and the lame.

When the crowd finally left, and the disciples sought their beds, and Jesus walked toward the hills, Matthias still followed; he could no more sleep than a child on a first journey to Jerusalem. When Jesus knelt to pray, Matthias dropped down beside a rock to wait for his friend, who had become the Master.

"Matthias!"

Matthias awoke, confused and groggy from the warm sun. Jesus was standing over him. He scrambled to his feet. "I didn't mean to disturb you," he stammered.

"You didn't." Jesus looked as rested as if he had slept all night. "What did you want of me, that you gave up a decent bed for a rock?" he asked, smiling.

At the question, awareness of his own need engulfed Matthias. He bowed his head. "Master . . ." Against his will his voice shook. "Will you . . . heal me too?"

In a quiet voice Jesus asked, "Remember the vow you made long ago to trust God?"

Startled, Matthias could only nod.

"Can you trust God now, accepting his will over your own?"

Matthias clamped his lips against crying out. Was healing his hand not God's will? He closed his eyes against the disappointment of giving up his dearest wish. When he opened them Jesus' look commanded an answer.

Matthias raised his chin and declared, "As God wills."

"As God wills," Jesus agreed. "Give me your hand."

From under his concealing robe, Matthias extended his left hand. It stretched out lithe and whole in the sun. Choking on sudden tears, he dropped to his knees. "My Lord! Oh, thank you. Thanks be to God!"

"Thanks be to the Father," Jesus said softly. He took Matthias's hands in his own, raised him to his feet, and embraced him. His cheeks were wet with tears too.

When Matthias could trust his voice, he said, "You've given me a new life! You've changed everything in an instant!" He held up his hand, flexing it and touching it in wonder.

Jesus cautioned, "God has even greater blessings than this for you, Matthias. Continue to trust him and do his will."

"I will!" exclaimed Matthias. How easy it would be now. He vowed, "These two hands are yours. I want only to serve you."

Jesus smiled the delighted, affectionate smile Matthias remembered so well from their boyhood. "Serve the Father, my friend. Nothing is greater than to serve God. And to serve him we must serve his children."

Those few simple words captivated Matthias. To serve God, one must serve people. He could do that. "Yes!" he exclaimed.

Then unexpectedly Jesus said, "I want you to go show your hand to your family. Show Shebuel too, but no one else in the holy city."

Matthias's impulse was to beg to stay—to tell them later, when going would not require separation from Jesus, but a servant wouldn't argue. "Shall I leave soon, Lord?"

Jesus nodded. "Yes. Go quickly." Before he could say more, shouts interrupted them.

"Here he is," one person called to another. Up the slope rushed a crowd. Simon pushed through to Matthias, bringing with him Joel, newly arrived from Jerusalem. The three made their way to the edge of the throng where they could talk.

Waving his hand in front of Simon, Matthias cried, "Look! Look! I'm healed!"

His friend grabbed his hand and held it up, marveling. "Healed! Of course!" He gave Matthias an exuberant hug.

Joel, wide eyed, asked hesitantly, "Sir . . . may I . . . touch it?"

Matthias squeezed his hand in a crushing grip.

Joel rubbed his pinched fingers. "You are healed!" he said, laughing.

"What can I not do with two hands?" Matthias challenged. He clasped them over his head, stretched them in the sun, and waved them, wanting to shout his news to everyone.

Then Joel remembered to tell Matthias that Shebuel was ill and begging to see him.

In Jerusalem at Shebuel's house, Matthias hurried to the old man's room. Shebuel, thin and white-haired, struggled to rise from his cushioned chair when Matthias entered. Before he could, Matthias rushed over and dropped to his knees in front of him.

He caught Shebuel's hands in his own and pressed his forehead against them before looking up. "Sir, how are you?"

Seeing two strong hands holding his own, Shebuel gaped. "Matthias!"

Matthias let go and leaned back on his heels. Turning his palms up, he flexed his fingers. "Jesus healed my hand."

Shebuel, trembling, grabbed the restored hand and turned it. "Healed! Healed by Jesus?"

"Yes, although it is by God's power. You can't imagine what I've witnessed since we last talked!"

"You must tell me! Everything!" the old man demanded. Then panting, he slumped back on his cushions.

Matthias jumped up. "Can I get you something?" Shebuel waved him off with a flutter of his bony hand. Shortly he murmured, "A little wine, please." Matthias snatched the flagon he indicated, poured some into a goblet, and held it to his lips. After a few sips, Shebuel motioned for him to set it back on the table. "I find myself weaker than I thought." He paused, panting. "Before I get too tired . . . I have a little business . . ." He reached behind his cushion and produced a small scroll. "Here. Read . . ."

Curious, Matthias sat on a chair opposite Shebuel and unrolled the scroll. It was a legal document addressed to him. He scanned it. Catching his breath, he read it again slowly. Shebuel had made him his sole heir and adopted son.

He bowed his head. He couldn't let the old man see his dismay. How could he serve Jesus and fulfill this responsibility? He wanted to cry out, no!

When Matthias looked up, Shebuel's sunken eyes had lost their anxious expression. His lined face had relaxed in contentment, and he showed no sign of perceiving Matthias's inner turmoil. This, more than his fragile appearance, told the younger man how ill he was, for in the past he often had seemed to read Matthias's very thoughts.

Now the old man beamed with simple pleasure. "I surprised you."

"Yes, you surely did, sir."

Shebuel's eyes brightened in their wreath of wrinkles. Hunching forward, he rearranged his cushions. "From the first day of your employment, you've been a son to me. Zibiah has known this and has been glad for me. Now you are her son too." He leaned back, drained by his burst of vigor.

Matthias could not say no. He took Shebuel's frail hand in his. "I am honored, sir."

Shebuel's eyes filled with tears. When he found his voice, he commanded, "Now, tell me about your wonderful healing."

Matthias obeyed, but the older man's fever-bright eyes worried him. Fearful he had excited Shebuel too much, he excused himself early.

Only after a night's sleep did the conflict of Matthias's situation fully grip him. He hadn't been able to say no to the merchant's gift. Yet how could he accept the responsibility of being the only son of an ailing old man?

He had vowed to serve Jesus. He really couldn't serve anyone else at the same time, not even his new father. He agonized over what to say to Shebuel.

After breakfast, Shebuel called him to his room and without preamble asked, "Will you return to Jesus?"

Matthias avoided the merchant's searching gaze. During his fitful night he'd thought of no way to please Shebuel and still serve Jesus. He couldn't get any words out.

Shebuel frowned. "You've never before found it difficult to be honest with me," he complained, petulant as a sick child. "Has adoption become a wall between us?"

Matthias dropped to his knees before the huddled shape his adoptive father had become. "Sir, never would I deceive you. It's just that I find it difficult to leave you . . . and I must."

The older man relaxed and placed his hand lightly on Matthias's head. "I had hoped to keep you here, but I'm content, knowing you are now my son wherever you are. If you must go to your teacher, then go with my blessing."

Matthias bowed his head under the gentle hand. "Thank you, sir. I am proud to be your son."

Later, however, while Matthias was making his way toward Emmaus, his duty to Shebuel plagued him. His adopted father, by releasing him so readily, had bound him more tightly.

When Matthias reached Emmaus, he relived the joy of his healing with his mother and grandmother. Their reactions—stunned at first, then weeping with happiness—rekindled his own awe. The God of Abraham, Isaac, and Jacob had visited them.

Back in Jerusalem he showed his hand to his family at the cheese shop, reveling in his newly acquired manual dexterity and strength until even Miriam began to smile at him as indulgently as a mother. The last thing he wanted from Miriam was mothering. More than ever, he desired her as a wife. The wholeness of his body made him feel like a boy again. It was as if loving and losing Elizabeth never had happened, and Miriam was his first love.

Nevertheless, he restrained himself in her presence. It was too soon to speak to Ethan. For even in times of war, a man was given a year to stay with his bride before going to battle. And Matthias couldn't wait a year to serve Jesus. He had made a vow.

The next day, on the heels of rejoicing, a painful message arrived at the house of Shebuel. Joel had not qualified for the School of Hillel. Matthias went to Neriah's office.

A troubled look crossed Neriah's face when Matthias walked in. He rose from his desk. "Matthias, I did the best I could for Joel. As I warned you, everything was against him."

"Surely not everything. His brilliance should have been enough, unless you let our personal differences dampen your enthusiasm," Matthias said brusquely.

Neriah's nostrils flared. "You are accusing me of lying?"

"You said it. Wear it if it fits."

"How dare you come in here, knowing nothing about the facts, and call me a liar? If it weren't for Elizabeth, I'd . . ."

"Forget Elizabeth. This is between you and me. Are you willing to break with your old ways and help Joel, or not?"

"I told you, I've done all I can. Matthias, please, let us remain friends."

Matthias glared at him, turned on his heel, and stormed out.

Seven

Grasping at the only hope left for Joel, Matthias went to ailing Rabbi Joash. Striding at the heels of a servant, he crossed the old man's courtyard, where even the vines looked ancient and weary of growing. The servant led him into a modest room where his former teacher lay, propped on pillows.

The rabbi raised his right hand. "My boy," he slurred. The left side of his mouth drooped, and his left eye stared, unresponsive to the smile that crinkled his right eye. "Come close, please."

Matthias knelt beside him. "Rabbi, it's good to see you."

"But not to see me like this, your face tells me."

Matthias had hoped his shock and distress wouldn't show.

"Be at peace, Matthias. I'm used to my portion. The Lord gives and the Lord takes. Blessed be the name of the Lord."

"Blessed be the name of the Lord," Matthias responded.

Joash studied him with a crooked smile. "Have you learned to obey your elders yet?"

"I hope so, sir."

"Then be seated comfortably and tell me about yourself."

Matthias told him that he had sold all to follow Jesus. He longed to show him his healed hand, but obediently kept it hidden. Finally, he told the revered rabbi about Joel, without implicating Neriah in the young man's rejection. "Please, sir," he concluded, "will you examine Joel and if you find him promising, intercede for him?"

"I'll do what I can, but I have little power at the academy these days."

"It is enough if you will speak for him, sir."

Encouraged by his visit with Rabbi Joash, Matthias went down the hill to the rug shop. While checking the accounts and inspecting the latest shipment, he had to remind himself to keep his healed hand concealed, for using it had become natural.

He and Tobias had just laid aside their tallying tablets when an outburst of derision rose above the normal shouts from the street. Matthias straightened. The shouts of contempt took him back to the streets of Nazareth, where his face had burned with shame each time the village boys had taunted him. It had taken him years to get over that unclean feeling.

Under the folds of his robe, he clenched his healed hand. Ultimately being crippled had strengthened him, but he'd never forgotten how it felt to need help. In quick, long strides Matthias reached the street, followed closely by Tobias. At sight of the two men, a cluster of boys fled. Matthias glanced to the right and the left, searching for the victim. "Well," he decided, "whoever it was must have escaped."

"It would seem so, sir," said Tobias with a relieved look.

Back inside the shop Matthias bent and untied the binding cord of one of the new carpets. Rich crimson, indigo, and saffron colors unfurled before him. "Hang this one by the door," he instructed. "Its beauty will entice buyers."

Tobias started to pick it up, but the scrape of sandals on the stone floor made them both turn around. A waist-high girl stared up at them with forlorn eyes. "Please . . . help me," she stammered. "I'm lost."

A livid welt on her cheek, smudges of dirt on the finely woven blue robe, and an embroidered hairband hanging around her neck told Matthias she was the missing victim.

Her self-control vanished and she began to sob. "I hid . . . in here . . . while you . . . chased them away!"

Having raised five sisters, Matthias knew what to do. He picked her up and held her close. When she stopped crying, he sat her atop a stack of carpets. "You're a brave girl. Now tell me what happened."

"Mushi let me look at jewelry while she went to the fishmonger's. Then I couldn't find her." A fresh sob choked her.

"Don't worry," he soothed. "You can't have wandered far." He studied her. Her wide, uptilted eyes and pointed chin reminded him of someone. He ran his fingers gently around the darkening bruise on her cheek. "Are you hurt anyplace else?"

She shook her head. "They made fun of my dress and my sandals. I pushed them and they pushed me against the potter's stall." She touched her cheek. "Then they shouted at me too."

For the first time Matthias noticed the well-made sandals on her feet, decorated with brass studs and colorful bits of glass. The street children ran barefoot, but some were not above stealing shoes from a little girl. He felt a twinge of anger at careless Mushi. "Whose daughter are you, little one?"

She raised her chin. "I'm the daughter of Neriah bar Elul."

"Neriah!" No wonder the eyes and face looked familiar.

"Do you know my father?" The girl's eyes glowed with pride.

"Yes, I certainly do."

"Then you can take me home!" Her cheek dimpled.

"Yes." He wasn't eager to see Neriah, but he probably wouldn't be home yet. "First, let me wash your face. If you go like this, you'll frighten your mother. Tobias, bring water, please." In a few moments he had her face sponged clean, her hair combed, and her hairband back in place.

"You didn't tell me your name," he said.

She smiled mischievously. "And you haven't told me yours."

"I am Matthias bar Aaron."

She hopped down from her perch on the rugs and bowed. "I am Anna Elizabeth," she said.

"Well, Anna Elizabeth, let's go quickly."

With her hand in his, he marched out and up the street. "You look for Mushi and tell me if you see her," he said. She saw no sign of her servant, so Matthias trudged toward the great houses in the upper city, trying to match his pace to hers. He'd intended to hand her over to Neriah's gatekeeper, but when they arrived she tugged him into the court, where a bevy of servants flocked around them. One ran to call Elizabeth.

She came to meet him, her face alight with surprise and pleasure. "Matthias!" Then she saw the girl's cheek and sobered. "Anna, what happened? Where is Mushi?"

At her concerned attention, Anna burst into tears again. While Elizabeth consoled her, her story tumbled out. After quieting Anna, Elizabeth sent two male servants to search for Mushi and sent the child to be bathed and dressed. To Matthias she said, "What a blessing she found you! It's incredible."

"The hand of God touches us all," he said.

She cast him a surprised glance, but her attention returned to her daughter. "I can't bear to think what might have happened. When Mushi returns . . . I've never wanted the servants punished, but I won't intercede for her this time."

"Your servant is undoubtedly suffering already for her carelessness," Matthias said gently. "She may even have had a mishap herself."

Her expression softened. "She does love Anna." Touching his arm, she said, "Thank you for reminding me. She probably is beside herself." Her fingers on his arm tightened. "Come. Let me offer you food and drink. I must do something to thank you."

She told her attendants to bring food and wine and led him to a cool guest room. Sitting opposite him at a small table, she said, "You calmed me when no one else could have."

"I only reminded you of what you already knew."

"But the Matthias I used to know would have been as angry as I was," she argued, smiling. "You have changed."

Oh, Elizabeth, if only I could tell you how much. He tightened the fingers of his healed hand, but kept it hidden in his lap.

The servants brought honeycakes. She served him and as they ate the years slipped away. They visited like youngsters again. Matthias, now so deeply in love with Miriam, could enjoy Elizabeth as a friend.

"You've sold everything to follow the Nazarene?" she gasped when he told her.

"Neriah didn't tell you? Yes. If you find me changed, it is because of Jesus."

"But . . . your mother and your grandmother . . ."

"Money from all that I sold is in their hands. And now . . . Shebuel has made me his son and heir."

"Oh, Matthias. How good of him." She reached across the narrow table between them and placed her hand over his. "Now you have the position and wealth you deserve."

"But it burdens me, because I've vowed to serve Jesus."

"How can Shebuel's wealth interfere with that?"

"He, his wife, and the business, all cry for my care. I have a son's responsibilities again. Yet I must live with Jesus as he lives, without home or family."

She squeezed his hand. "You will do what is best. I wish I could know your friend Jesus."

"Oh, Elizabeth, if only you could." He forgot himself and clasped her hand in both of his. Remembering too late, he let go and dropped his hands to his lap under the edge of the table.

But she had felt and glimpsed two strong hands.

She stood up slowly. "Matthias. Your hand. What happened to your hand?"

He rose to face her, his left hand safely hidden in the folds of his robe. He couldn't lie to her, so he said nothing.

She stepped around the table. "Let me see it," she persisted.

When he didn't respond, she drew back the sleeve of his robe and uncovered his hand.

"Oh, Matthias," she murmured. "It is whole . . . and strong!" Tears sprang to her eyes. She lifted his hand and pressed it to her cheek. "You've been healed!" She threw her arms around him, weeping and laughing at the same time.

He laughed with her, glad that she knew. "Jesus healed me. You see now why I owe him everything." He embraced her lightly for only a moment, but it was a moment too long.

"They told me I'd find you here," Neriah's voice came coldly from the doorway.

"Neriah!" exclaimed Elizabeth. "I just . . ."

"Go to your quarters," he snapped.

"But . . ."

"Go, before I publicly denounce you!"

"Neriah," Matthias interceded. "It's not what you think." To save Elizabeth, he held out his left hand. "Look. I've been healed. She was rejoicing that I've been healed."

Neriah stared. The look on his face shifted from rage to astonishment and back to anger. "And you had to rush here to show my wife after concealing it from me?" he accused.

"No, no, Neriah," said Elizabeth. "Anna was lost in the city and he brought her home."

This new information only enraged Neriah more. "Go to your room!" he shouted.

With bowed head, she obeyed.

"And you! Get out of my house!" he yelled at Matthias. Whirling on his heel, he went after his wife.

Matthias left quickly, cursing himself for a fool. He knew better than to linger with Elizabeth, let alone touch her. Nothing would soften Neriah's wrath toward him. He could only pray the man would not be harsh with Elizabeth.

Having revealed his healed hand to the nephew of Caiaphas, against Jesus' instructions, Matthias could only guess at the consequences, but Neriah probably would use his power against Jesus, as well as against Matthias.

As quickly as possible Matthias found Joel and told him Rabbi Joash would summon him. He took his leave of Shebuel and Zibiah, and he hurried to the house above the cheese shop.

Miriam answered his impatient knock. "Matthias!" Then she noticed his rough garb and her smile faded. "You're going back to Galilee? I thought you'd stay and return to Shebuel's business . . . now that you are his son . . ."

He drank in the vision of her upturned face, her burnished hair fastened modestly under a light veil, her lips parted, inviting. "Does it matter to you that I leave, or are you only concerned for Shebuel?" It was a question befitting a callow boy, but his desire for her made him feel as uncertain as a youth.

She lowered her gaze. "Of course I care."

He stepped close and tipped her chin up. "Look at me, Miriam," he whispered.

She caught his hand and pressed her forehead against it. When she raised her eyes, it was as if she had thrown aside a veil.

He kissed her fingers and clasped her hand to his chest. "I love you so much, Miriam." The words burst out unbidden.

"And I love you," she cried. "Please . . . don't go away again."

"Dearest Miriam. My beloved." He caught her in a rough embrace and rubbed his cheek against her hair as her mantle slipped back. She yielded, slipping her arms around his waist.

Coming to himself, he released her. "I wanted so much to see you alone, but I never dreamed . . . that you would really . . . Oh, Miriam," he groaned, "how can I leave you now?"

"Stay, then," she urged happily, "and help Shebuel and speak to Father." She stopped, realizing he had not mentioned marriage.

He started to reassure her, but his declaration caught in his throat. For the present he could not marry. He was nothing, could offer her nothing, if he failed to serve his Master first.

She misinterpreted his hesitation. Her face burned with embarrassment as she backed away. "I see I've misunderstood." She ran inside.

"No! Miriam! Let me explain!" he called, but she had disappeared. Reluctantly he retreated down the steps and entered the cheese shop, where he made his farewell to Cleopas, Ethan, Hannah, and even the children, but Miriam refused to see him again.

Eight

Returning to Jesus, who was preaching near Nain, was like coming home again. The Master showed no concern over Neriah or his uncle, the high priest. So Matthias put them out of his own mind as well.

Matthias's sorrow over having left Miriam without being able to reassure her eased as he watched for ways to serve his Master. He made certain Jesus never hungered or thirsted while he preached to the multitudes throughout Galilee. When the nights grew cooler Matthias hiked back to Capernaum to fetch a woolen cloak for Jesus. He shepherded the throngs to give space to the Master when he wanted to move. And he used his merchant's skill at persuasion on those who tried to follow the Lord when he retired to pray.

Then as the crowds grew even greater, Matthias could discover no way to protect his Master's rest. And when the Pharisees' anger against the Nazarene increased, Matthias again feared for Jesus' safety.

Winter dragged on. With each passing day, Matthias missed Miriam more. Only a fool would fall into daydreaming of a copper-haired woman while he served the Master. Yet as if she were a part of himself, he couldn't escape his need for her.

Finally, just when winter seemed entrenched forever, the first warm breezes of spring wafted over the lake. Crimson lilies marched up Galilee's hills. Blue-and-white iris and knee-high narcissi waved at the sea. Slopes rippled with purple anemones, blue hyacinths, and pink cyclamens. Fields of yellow mustard collided with ravines of pink oleanders. In such a place, in the company of the Master, no evil seemed possible. Matthias relaxed his vigil. Only the presence of Miriam could have added to his happiness.

As if in answer to his wish, Jesus led them back to the holy city for Passover. Jerusalem was a welcome sight to Matthias and to Judas Iscariot, who had grown a little homesick. At the city gate Judas asked, "Will you stay with Shebuel?"

"Yes. I'll meet all of you in the temple each day."

"I wish I could stay with my friend Lemuel. But right now, he bitterly disapproves of what he calls my penchant for following dreams and dreamers. And his tongue is sharp."

"Too bad. I'm glad Shebuel sympathizes with my desires."

"You are blessed to have such a mentor."

"Yes." Uncomfortable over Judas's undisguised envy, Matthias fell silent.

The disciples formed pairs to progress up the congested street. Strolling beside Matthias, Judas remarked, "I wonder if Jesus thinks Shebuel may be of value to the coming Kingdom."

Puzzled, Matthias asked, "What do you mean?"

Judas grinned. "You know as well as I that money speaks in certain places. Shebuel has a goodly amount. And after all, you told me Jesus sent you back to him at just the right moment for your adoption."

"Yes, but he certainly didn't . . ."

Judas burst into laughter. His face reflected boyish glee at Matthias's distress.

"You speak in jest," Matthias accused.

"Of course!" Judas continued to chuckle and Matthias joined him.

During the first days of the Feast of Unleavened Bread, nothing occurred in the way Matthias had hoped. Although he saw Miriam, and she confirmed by her behavior that she had forgiven him, he could not talk to her privately. And Jesus, by healing a lame man on the Sabbath, enraged members of the Sanhedrin. Fearing the penalty—stoning—for breaking the Sabbath, Matthias tried desperately to keep his body between Jesus and his accusers.

On the morning of the fourth feast day, when the holiest days had passed, Shebuel called Matthias into the small dining room where Zibiah was laying out a simple repast of unleavened bread and dried dates. Shebuel said in an uneasy voice, "I heard that important Pharisees have accused Jesus of breaking the Sabbath."

"Yes, sir. I was with him when he healed the lame man."

Shebuel said shakily, "I feared this could happen. Their anger will grow with each day Jesus remains here." The older man's face softened. "He is a good man . . . a brilliant man. Too bad that his work may be cut short."

"You truly believe he's in danger?"

Shebuel reared up from his cushions. "Have you forgotten what Annas did to you, an insignificant young student? Although Caiaphas is now high priest, he is of the same mind. Actually, Annas remains the real power behind his nephew."

Without question, the high priest had empowered Neriah to do as he wished against Matthias. And Matthias's memory remained all too vivid. Even now a twinge of outrage pricked him again.

Shebuel continued. "Jesus may rouse Rome's fear of a popular uprising. If they doubt the ability of our Jewish rulers to keep order, they will remove them and put Romans over us. If I can see this, surely the high priest can. Furthermore, Jesus may now have given the Sanhedrin legal grounds to do away with him."

Recalling the faces of the priests and members of the Sanhedrin when they had accused Jesus of breaking the Sabbath, Matthias realized Shebuel was right. He nodded, his mind racing ahead. There must be some way to turn aside this growing threat. Not wanting to involve his adopted father in his plans, he ate hurriedly, excused himself, and sent Joel with a message to Reuben.

By the sixth hour, Matthias was pacing the floor in a spacious reception room of the house of Joed. Before he could sit, Reuben appeared, followed by his father. Reuben looked leaner than ever, and Judah ben Joed's square shoulders had begun to sag. Matthias took Reuben's extended hand and bowed to the older man.

"Matthias!" cried Judah. "How happy we were to hear about your hand!" The older man embraced him, and then grasped his restored left hand. "How wonderful for you," he said, lifting it up into the lamplight for a closer look.

"Yes, sir."

Judah peered into Matthias's face. "Incredible!" he exclaimed. "What did he do to heal it like that?"

"Why . . . in a way he didn't do anything. He asked me if I trusted God, and then he asked me to reach forth my hand. When I did, it was whole."

"Then the Nazarene did not really heal you."

"His power is from God. God healed me."

Judah's face assumed a closed look. "Who knows the source of his power? But let us not argue. Be seated and tell me what we can do for you." Judah gestured to a chair and took one beside it.

As briefly as possible, Matthias explained his concern following the episode of the Sabbath healing. "Sir, Jesus is a righteous man, who reveres the Law. I came to ask mercy for him."

Judah's eyes narrowed. Moistening his lips with his tongue, he asked, "Surely you don't think I can grant that?"

"You might influence others to calm the Sanhedrin."

"You ask the impossible!" Suddenly fear widened his eyes. He stood abruptly. Matthias scrambled to his feet and turned toward the open door in time to see a familiar retreating figure. Neriah had appeared unannounced.

Judah, without a farewell, hurried after his son-in-law.

Laying a hand on Matthias's shoulder, Reuben said, "I'm sorry. If I'd known the nature of your request, I could have spared both you and him. Father couldn't get into a controversy over the Nazarene even if he wanted to. Just by entertaining you, he risks alienation from Neriah."

The embers of Matthias's old anger exploded into flames. He stalked to the doorway and glowered down the empty hallway.

Reuben followed at his heels.

Matthias ground out, "So Neriah controls the house of Joed."

"Please," Reuben urged. "Be seated and let me explain."

Matthias returned and threw himself in a chair.

Reuben began, "For Father even to welcome you, after what you did . . ." He waved aside Matthias's attempted protest. "I know . . . Elizabeth told me. But knowing Neriah's jealousy, I can't imagine how you . . . He's made her a prisoner in her own home since you were there."

"The beast! She's innocent of any wrongdoing!"

"According to the Law he could cast her out," Reuben reminded him. "At least he hasn't done that. She still has her home and her children."

"And there's nothing I can do," Matthias groaned.

"Just stay away. I'm sure that in time Neriah's love for her will win out and he will reinstate her. But you can see Father's position. He's no longer young and he wants harmony with the father of his grandchildren. For that matter, he wants no problems with Caiaphas either."

In frustration Matthias strode back to the open door.

Reuben matched his pace, step for step. "Matthias . . . as for your friend Jesus . . . I told you to warn him. He has become a target for the powerful."

Matthias pushed his hair back and pressed his fingers against his eyes. The old hatred tore at him. Neriah was unjustly persecuting Elizabeth, and intuition told him the Pharisee would just as viciously try to harm Jesus. He lowered his hand and blinked. "I did warn Jesus. He doesn't see any danger. Why else do you think I would come here for help? I believed your father to be a fair man, in spite of how he gave Elizabeth to Neriah and refused to listen to my side . . ." He squared his shoulders and swung around to confront Reuben. "What about you? Does Neriah control you too?"

Reuben's lips curved with wry humor. "He knows that with or without his pleasure, I will see my sister and choose my friends. But," he added carefully, "I have made my peace with him. I hope you can again."

"Peace!" Matthias spat. "How does one make peace with a wild dog who turns his teeth against his own?"

With raised brows, Reuben countered, "Perhaps you could guess that better than I. You are as hotheaded as he is, and you both hold onto grudges beyond reason."

Matthias glowered. "He keeps giving me new reasons to despise him!" He stepped out into the hall to leave.

Reuben grabbed him by the arm. "Matthias, he's always feared you more than he has hated you."

Matthias forced a laugh. "A dog bites as hard, whichever the reason!" He pulled away.

Reuben sighed. "Between you and that Zealot Simon, I'm inclined to think Nazarenes deserve their reputations."

"One Nazarene doesn't!" Matthias flashed back.

"Your Jesus, of course."

"Yes." At the thought of Jesus, Matthias's anger cooled. "Reuben, you've got to meet him! I believe he is the . . ." He stopped. Without realizing it, he almost had said too much. "He is like no one else," he finished lamely.

"When I saw your hand, I knew that."

"I would do anything for him. That's why I came here," said Matthias. Just remembering the Master calmed him. He caught Reuben staring at him with an odd look.

Before either could speak, Neriah appeared again in the hall.

"Good evening, Brother," Reuben called.

Matthias said nothing. His moment of peace fled.

Neriah muttered good night to Reuben, but kept his eyes on Matthias.

His glance dropped to Matthias's healed left hand, and his eyes hardened. "Disciple of a blasphemer. How suitable for a seducer of women." His voice rose. "How dare you come to this house?"

More than anything in the world, Matthias wanted to feel his fist smashing Neriah's thick lips against his teeth. His thought must have shown on his face, for Neriah spun around and left.

Matthias ground out, "If you will excuse me, Reuben, I shall go also. Please extend my apologies to your father. Assure him I will never again impose upon him."

Reuben went with him to the gate. He said, "I want you to know, you've convinced me Jesus is not a false prophet. At the first opportunity I shall go to hear him."

Matthias clapped him on the shoulder. "It was worth coming here tonight just to hear you say that."

As Matthias pushed his way through the crowds of Passover worshipers in the upper city, he wondered who else could influence the Sanhedrin. He thought of Nicodemus, but dismissed him as too secretive.

He could think of no way to soften the opposition of the Jewish rulers.

If Shebuel were correct, the Master would be safer in Galilee. Although the high priest's power extended that far, in a practical sense it did not. If only Jesus would stay there until he was established in the hearts of the people, he could sweep into the holy city with so much popular backing no one would dare to harm him.

Somehow Matthias must persuade Jesus to leave Jerusalem immediately. Yet how could the servant lead the Master?

Nine

The next day, to Matthias's surprise and joy, Ethan unwittingly gave him an opportunity to talk privately with Miriam. When Matthias arrived at the house above the cheese shop, Cleopas and his family were gone and Ethan was leaving. "Daughter, I leave you to make Matthias welcome," he said and left by the door Matthias had entered. In his absence the room seemed suddenly larger and very quiet.

When Matthias greeted Tamara she smiled a motherly welcome and then graciously poured water for him to wash. "You must be hungry," she said as she handed him a towel. Her broad face beamed. "Miriam, stay with your guest. I will prepare it." She glided ponderously from the room.

With a delighted smile, Miriam led him to a cushion beside a small table. "When she gets like that, I can only obey her."

"You were not this agreeably obedient as a child," he teased.

She settled on a cushion across from him, tucking her feet sideways and smoothing her white robe over them. The blue-and-green border of her mantle fell in a graceful cascade from her hair to her shoulders to her wrists.

Laughing, she said, "All the more reason I should humor Tammy now. She's been a mother to me." In a quieter voice, meant only for him, she added, "As with any mother, wouldn't she know how I longed to be alone with you for a few moments?"

"Oh, Miriam. It grieved me beyond words to leave you last time with such a misunderstanding. I walked the hills of Galilee with my heart aching for you."

She glanced at him and then down at her hands folded in her lap. "I tried to put you out of my mind. I even encouraged the attentions of Hiram . . ."

"Who is Hiram?" he interrupted.

"A young man who has spoken to Father for me."

"Are you betrothed?" he gasped.

She shook her head and raised her chin. "Father has promised to consider my wishes, and I don't want to marry Hiram."

Matthias sighed in relief. "Praise be to Jehovah for making Ethan a merciful man." It was on the tip of his tongue to beg her to marry him, but he caught himself. He was less free now than before, for Jesus had warned everyone they must love him more than their own families if they were to be his disciples.

Miriam waited expectantly.

His silence grew into a wall between them.

She looked away, frowning.

"Miriam, it is . . . I've made a vow before God to serve Jesus as a bondservant until he . . . I can't marry now, but a day will come when I . . . when we . . ."

The scuffing sound of Tamara's sandals announced her return. She placed a dish of sweet bread and cheese between them and left.

Matthias went on hurriedly, "You weren't presuming when you suggested betrothal. But I am presuming to mention it, when I can't fulfill the duties of a bridegroom."

She blushed, but with her usual candidness asked, "What then are we to do?"

Tamara appeared again, placed wine and cups, and left.

Miriam's eyes probed his in a disconcerting way. Her directness when she was small had charmed him. Now, although many would think it unwomanly, her keen intellect and straightforward speech excited him.

"With all my heart I want to ask for you," he whispered. "But I can't pledge myself. I must leave my fate in your hands, knowing that you, as a woman, may not be able to do anything for either of us."

She answered slowly, "I told you, Father has given me a say."

Matthias knew Miriam's hold on such freedom was tenuous. Even though Ethan had permitted her to be educated contrary to custom, he sometimes seemed at a loss to know what to do with his uniquely gifted daughter. Aloud Matthias cautioned, "It is hard to stand alone against the ways of men and women. Like any righteous Jew, your father eagerly awaits the blessing of grandchildren. He may decide he must go ahead and marry you to someone soon."

"No! He has always granted me privileges. Most men would say it was a mistake to encourage a woman's desire to learn, but not my father." Contrary to the assurance of her words, she looked so vulnerable . . . so alone against traditions as strong as the Law.

"It's hard for you to be different from other women," he said, surprised the thought hadn't come to him sooner.

She poured wine into the two cups and handed him one. "Please ask the blessing," she said.

He raised the cup, said the prayer, and waited for her to drink.

She held her cup in both hands and stared into it. Just when he thought she was going to ignore his last comment, she said, "Sometimes I wish I didn't think so much and question so much." With her chin down and her eyes shielded by the dark crescents of her lashes, she said, "You've always helped me, Matthias. You've never resented my arguing or my need to know. Why has my learning not bothered you, like it has other men?"

"Your mind has always delighted me, from the time I first met that little red-haired girl who used to swing on my arm. To me you are more than a woman or a scholar. You are . . . Miriam," he concluded simply. Her name encompassed everything he loved.

He must have said the right thing. Her smile was like sunlight.

Suddenly cheerful and relaxed, she volunteered, "About Hiram . . . I've known him since I was a child. He lives nearby. Now that he is a temple guard, he's become overbearing. I really wish he'd leave me alone."

Matthias scowled. The thought of a brawny temple guard forcing his attentions upon Miriam roused instant anger. "If he troubles you, you must tell Ethan!"

"Father likes Hiram . . . thinks he is honorable, as well as ambitious . . ."

"But surely he wouldn't want you to be made uncomfortable."

"Father and Cleopas think I make much of nothing. And perhaps I do. I just don't like how he looks at me or how he talks to me."

"I'll speak to Cleopas. You shouldn't have to endure this man's attentions if he is distasteful to you."

"I think I should speak for myself," she asserted.

Knowing her independent spirit, he could only agree. "But promise you won't allow Hiram to intimidate you."

"Of course. I shall not permit anything I do not wish."

He laughed at the familiar lift of her chin. "I don't fear for you when you look like that!"

Sooner than he could believe, the mealtime had passed. With regret he excused himself and rose to his feet. "I must go now to meet Jesus."

Miriam rose, her brow creasing with anxiety. "Matthias, Rabbi Ebed says the Nazarene is a false Messiah . . . that he will confuse people and finally be put down as they all have been."

"Do you believe that, Miriam?"

"I don't know," she admitted. "Rabbi is so wise and has seen so much. Except for you, I think I would believe him. Who do you think Jesus is?"

"I can't tell you yet what I truly think about Jesus. But his works speak for him. No man ever has done what he is doing." He held out his left hand. "Could a common man do that?"

"But you said God had healed you."

"He did, through Jesus."

"I don't know what to think . . ."

He took her hand in both of his own. Its smallness surprised him anew. She appeared so strong, yet felt so fragile. "One day you will know. Go ahead and question and listen and learn. In the end you'll agree with me."

Her fingers tightened on his. "Is your life with him all you had hoped it would be?"

"More than I'd hoped or could imagine. Each day brings miracles of healing and truths so piercing they shake the foundations of all I've ever learned . . . but there's more . . ."

Her nearness distracted him. He released her hand and stepped back. "I don't know how to say it, but the overwhelming thing is Jesus' love for people. I sometimes think he would give his life for the cripples he heals. It's almost as if he'd like to take their place and put on their filthy rags. I can see it in his eyes . . . in the way he touches them." He hesitated and then concluded, "Many of the poor see him as I see him and worship him."

In a startled voice she asked, "Do you worship him, Matthias?"

He understood her concern. Unlike the Gentiles, no Israelite dared to worship a man. Yet . . . "I suppose if I am honest, I would have to admit, yes. I too worship him."

He could see shock run through her. "But he is only a man, even if a good man!"

"He's more than a good man." He groped for words. "What he is, I'm not sure, but I would gladly die for him. Until that time, I live to serve him."

"Matthias," she choked out, "you are beside yourself! Your healing and your affection for this Nazarene have made you forget the first commandment!" She raised trembling fingers to her lips as if in saying it aloud, she had made matters worse.

"I see more clearly than ever before, and I understand the Law as never before," he assured her. He glanced around, searching for a glimpse of Tamara. Seeing they were still alone, he leaned over and swiftly kissed Miriam on the forehead. "I must go. Please thank Tamara for me . . . for us." Before she could respond he went to the door and let himself out.

She followed quickly and stood in the doorway. He wanted to hold her close and kiss the anxiety from her face. Instead he kept his hands clamped to his sides. Uncertainty was their lot. To let her think otherwise would be unfair.

Shaking inwardly at the strength of his desire for her, he blurted, "Goodbye," and hurried down to the alley. When he glanced back, she was still standing rooted to the top step.

To Matthias's relief, his Master already had decided to leave the holy city with the rest of the country people who were going back home. Matthias did not disclose the facts of his unsuccessful effort to enlist Judah ben Joed's help, but he did tell Jesus about Shebuel's fears.

Jesus only remarked, "Your adopted father is a wise and righteous man."

Back in Galilee, the disciples returned to the familiar routines surrounding their teacher's ministry.

Matthias, relieved at first to have put distance between himself and those who might distract him from his vow to serve Jesus, found himself still troubled. He began to see the threat of Neriah's bitter opposition in every arrogant Pharisee who confronted Jesus and to wonder if any of them, like bar Elul, had the ear of Caiaphas.

In addition to this, concern for Shebuel nagged at him.

And Miriam—always the longing for Miriam. Sometimes he let himself drift into dreams of marrying her just as he was, a wandering disciple of the Master. Then in despair, he would force his thoughts elsewhere. Even if she believed in Jesus, this was no life for a bride. Later, when the Kingdom was established . . . But when he allowed himself to consider that promised day, he was filled with dread that she already would be wed to someone else.

Only while he served the Master in some special way did Matthias find peace.

As the days turned to weeks and the weeks to months, however, threats against Jesus seemed to build like the storm clouds that gather power on mountaintops. Twice more the Pharisees accused the Master of breaking the Sabbath. The second time Matthias detected a streak of hysteria in their rage. Later he saw them huddled furtively with some of Herod's officers. After that he doubled his watchfulness, listening even to the gossip of the crowds.

One morning the sun rose high, burning away the shade, but the Master did not return from his night of prayer. Having protectively followed Jesus a short distance, Matthias could guess where he might be. So now he led the disciples up the path Jesus had climbed. When they found him he gathered them around and chose twelve men, whom he called Apostles, to be his special messengers. Matthias was not one of the Twelve.

At first the selection of the Apostles did not change anything for Matthias. Then Jesus began to teach the Twelve privately. When Jesus didn't need Matthias he felt useless. He tried, but couldn't rid himself of a shameful feeling of being left out. Loneliness dogged him. He cast about for more work to do. Work always had lifted his spirit. At last it struck him that he could serve Jesus by serving the Twelve.

Once he thought about it, the challenge to see what he could do for all those sturdy Galileans—and the Judean, Iscariot—made him chuckle.

Because Miriam was always in his thoughts, he tried to imagine her reaction to his idea, but could not. Would she understand the humility that Jesus taught? Would she ever share his belief in Jesus? He wished he could match wits with her and persuade her to believe.

Longing for her possessed him. If only he could feast his eyes upon her and dwell in the music of her laughter during the times when Jesus went off alone with the Apostles.

For the first time doubt pricked him. Had he made the right decision—to leave everything to follow Jesus? For that matter, did Jesus really want him in Galilee?

Ten

The day came when Jesus sent the Apostles out by twos to preach and to heal people in his name, but he didn't need Matthias. So with the westerly winds bringing showers, and nights growing colder, Matthias returned alone to Capernaum.

For several weeks he helped some of the families of the Twelve prepare for winter. Then he gained work as an ironsmith. Wrestling iron with two good hands, instead of one as he had learned to do with his father in Nazareth, gave him a sensuous joy. His back and arms grew strong and hard with new muscle.

From time to time he heard that Jesus had preached in some distant town, and he looked forward to being reunited with him. But in the month of Tebet, as the days lengthened, Matthias was overwhelmed by such a need to see Miriam that he felt ill. No amount of hammering eased his hunger for her. Knowing he could go and return easily before Passover, he rolled up an extra woolen robe to shield against the still sharp wind of the mountains and set out for the holy city.

Shebuel and Zibiah welcomed him with a festive supper. Their house guest Joel, who had finally entered the School of Hillel, did not come home in time for the celebration, but Zibiah explained that he seldom came home, except to sleep.

At last the old couple excused themselves and retired.

Night had conquered the last vestige of daylight by the time Matthias walked alone to the house above the cheese shop. A cold moon shone through a gap in the clouds, and then slipped away again, leaving stark blackness beyond the glow of his torch.

The thought of seeing Miriam sent his heart racing like a boy's. At her door his knees threatened to fail him. He greeted everyone as breathlessly as if he had been running, and at last turned to Miriam. "And how are your studies coming?" he asked soberly.

"Very well," she replied, letting her smile say more than her words could.

Tamara, who had slipped away, appeared with warmed wine and honey cakes and bade them sit to be served. In happy family custom, they sat in a large circle on mats and cushions.

"Tell us about Jesus," said Cleopas.

"He has healed more people than I can number. He even healed a leper." While Matthias spoke, his eyes rested on Miriam. He tried to memorize afresh the arch of her brows, the tilt of her sea-green eyes, and the delicate line of her nose.

"A leper!" she exclaimed. "He made a leper clean?"

"Clean as a newborn babe," said Matthias.

"Not since Elisha has a prophet cleansed a leper," said Ethan with awe.

Cleopas leaned forward in excitement. "What does he say now about the Kingdom?"

"He says the Kingdom is near. Yet he speaks of love, not rebellion. He says if we love God, we must also love all men, even our enemies."

Cleopas's mouth fell open. "Love our enemies! But the Law says we should exact punishment equal to the crime—an eye for an eye. Are we to forget justice . . . ignore what Rome has done to us . . . turn our backs on their abuse of innocent people?"

"Jesus says God desires mercy and forgiveness."

Ethan cleared his throat noisily. To Cleopas he said, "My son, I've waited a lifetime to hear about this kind of love."

"But Father," said Miriam, "Rabbi Ebed says we must not ignore evil. And Rome knows only the sword. Does Jesus expect us to conquer Romans by embracing them?"

"Hush, daughter," commanded Ethan. He leaned over and touched Matthias's hand. "Tell me more."

Matthias tried to make his own words as clear and simple as the words of his Master. "Jesus says we should love our enemies as much as we love ourselves. If someone slaps us across one cheek, we ought to turn the other. If a Roman forces us to walk a mile with him, we should freely give him a second mile of service."

Cleopas exclaimed, "But this would enslave us more. For the first time, I doubt your Master's wisdom."

Ethan shook his head. "You're too hasty, Son. Go on, Matthias. I would hear more."

Miriam, with a perplexed frown, listened silently.

Matthias continued until Ethan stood up painfully to stretch.

In spite of their protests, Matthias came to his feet also and excused himself. When he bade farewell to Miriam, only her lips smiled. She had been so quiet. He yearned to speak with her alone.

On his way home the streets were empty. He heard distant shouts of Roman soldiers harassing some hapless Jew. As Matthias turned the corner into his own street, a group of husky men, four abreast, confronted him with torches held high, forcing him to make way for the wealthy man they escorted.

The man in their center gestured them aside and approached Matthias. From the shadowed hood the familiar voice of Neriah cut like a lash. "So it is you. What is your so-called Master doing in the holy city now? Or have you regained your senses and deserted him?"

"He's not here, nor have I left him," Matthias replied.

"Ha! Vultures flocking to carrion are cleaner than the likes of you, running after a wonder worker who despises the Law." The armed servants edged closer, but Neriah motioned them away and turned his back on Matthias. With military precision, the group marched on up the street.

Well, at least Neriah no longer walks alone at night. I wonder what evil led him across my path at this unlikely hour.

The encounter left Matthias edgy. When he stepped inside Shebuel's gate and heard the keeper lock it, he breathed easier, though he knew the sense of security it offered was false. If Jesus were here he would say, stone walls provide no sanctuary. God alone protects.

After a night's sleep the chance meeting with Neriah faded to insignificance. At breakfast when Matthias told Shebuel more of Jesus' teaching, the old man said, "You are blessed, my son, to sit at this man's feet, but I fear for Israel." The lines on his face deepened. "How many of God's prophets has Israel welcomed?"

Matthias nodded. The Jews had ignored and killed their prophets. "But none before can compare to Jesus," he argued. "Surely our people cannot help but see God's favor on him."

Shebuel stroked his gray beard without comment.

Matthias waited respectfully, but the older man was lost in contemplation. Closing his eyes, he began to rock forward and back. His lips moved in silent prayer.

Matthias eased his sandaled feet across the marble floor and left. On the way to the rug shop, he thought about Miriam's troubled look the night before. Had Ethan's rebuke upset her? She ordinarily spoke when she wished, and her father let her. Thinking back, Matthias finally recalled her shock at hearing Jesus' charge to love one's enemies. Of course! Forgiving an enemy had troubled her as much as it had Cleopas. It was difficult to consider loving a Roman or a Samaritan . . . or Neriah.

Neriah's name had popped up unbidden. Matthias slowed his steps, ignoring shoppers who pushed to get around him. *Oh, Lord, how can I love Neriah?* He halted as though in chains.

From his memory leaped scene after scene—Neriah contemptuous, threatening, abusive, vengeful, and powerful. The man deserved retribution. Matthias pounded his fist against the palm of his left hand as if it were his enemy. With the jolt of the impact, he stopped and stared at his restored hand. *How can I think of raising this hand God healed against another man . . . even Neriah?*

In remorse, he opened his hands, palms up, and whispered, "Oh, God of our Fathers, forgive me. Help me!" Had he not been in the street, he would have dropped to his knees, so unbearable was the weight of his guilt. He'd been so sure of himself, thinking he was serving the Lord. He had expected Miriam and Cleopas to accept Jesus' word when he himself had not.

He stalked on, ashamed and defeated. If the Master could speak to him now, what would he say?

"Whatever you wish others would do for you, do that for them."

Yes! Jesus had said that over and over in many ways. In this manner a man might love . . . even an enemy. *What would I want? I guess I'd want the friendship that made us brothers back in the beginning.*

But that's impossible, he argued with himself.

No, it's not. Ask his forgiveness.

I tried that. I can't! Oh, God, help me!

Take him an exceedingly pleasing gift. This last came like a thought superimposed upon his own. Although he hadn't thought of it in years, he remembered the exquisite harp Neriah had given him when they both were students in the School of Hillel. How it had cheered him to learn the young Pharisee had searched diligently for an instrument he could play with one hand. Perhaps, with God's help, he could initiate peace with such a gesture of goodwill.

He turned in his tracks, went back to Shebuel, and withdrew a portion of his own money. Then he went to the man who had sold precious manuscripts to Shebuel and bargained for his most prized scroll of the Torah. Only a scholar such as Neriah could read the beloved Law in ancient Hebrew.

Back in his apartment he selected a small treasure of his own—a chest from Shebuel. The scroll and chest together would honor any rabbi. Matthias smoothed and retied the linen wrapping on the scroll and placed it reverently in the chest.

That evening Matthias knocked on Neriah's gate. A young male servant led him to a guest hall off the empty, quiet courtyard.

Neriah appeared in moments. He snarled, "Couldn't you wait until morning to come here begging?"

"What I came for is worthy of all speed," Matthias answered, refusing to be thrown off by insults. "I want to say I'm sorry I've offended you in the worst way . . . and to beg your forgiveness. I wish we could be friends. As a token of my esteem, I bring you this." He placed the carved chest in a startled Neriah's hands.

Perhaps the only thing that prevented Neriah from throwing it on the stone paving was his recognition that it held a holy scroll. He tried to give it back. Matthias backed away.

"Do you think you can buy a position for your slave boy?" spat Neriah. "I told you he was not fit for the academy."

"What are you talking about?"

"No amount of bribery will get Joel back into the academy."

"Joel is out of the academy?" Matthias exclaimed.

Neriah's mouth twisted with contempt. "Like you, he demonstrated weakness of character."

The desire for forgiveness that Matthias had nursed prayerfully vanished like dew before a desert wind. "You liar! Son of liars! Joel is honorable and righteous. Have you set out to do him ill because of me? Rabbi Joash will hear of this."

"So your honorable Joel has neglected to tell you Joash died two months ago," Neriah sneered.

Matthias's grief for the wise old rabbi was instant, but the news about Joel required his immediate action. Joel had not been home in two days.

As if reading his thoughts, Neriah said, "You'll find your slave boy with the dirty beggars at the Gennath Gate. He thinks more of them than he does of his teachers."

Matthias stalked out, leaving in Neriah's hands the scroll in its handsome chest. It was a small pleasure to note the frustrated frown on Neriah's face as he glanced down at the gift.

When the shock from the news about Joel and Joash subsided, Matthias realized the extent of his own failure. Rather than loving an enemy, he despised Neriah more than ever. In contrition, he clenched his fists. "Oh God, my God!" he groaned. His only hope lay in Jesus. The Master could save him from himself, just as he had healed his hand. But Jesus was in Galilee.

Eleven

Matthias searched for Joel until evening. If the beggars around the Gennath Gate knew him, they remained close-lipped. Finally Matthias gave up. His tired feet led him toward the cheese shop and the one person in the city who could cheer him.

Holding his cloak closed, he leaned into the wind and almost missed seeing Miriam standing by a food vendor's stall. He swerved toward her, and then realized she was talking with a tall man. No harm in joining them, he decided.

He dodged around a cart, and when he looked up, Miriam was only a pace away. Her flashing eyes signaled a problem. The man, strikingly handsome in a swarthy way, wore the uniform of a temple guard. He must be Hiram, the one she didn't like. With arrogant familiarity, the guard took possession of her arm.

She pulled away.

Matthias stepped between them, fury clouding his vision.

"Matthias!" Miriam cried. She grabbed his arm with both hands. "It's all right. This is Hiram. He meant no harm." But her voice was shaking.

Hiram, who had held his ground, retreated a pace, smiling. "Indeed I did not. Miriam and I are . . . old friends."

"If you are a friend, you will never again force your attentions on her," warned Matthias.

With boyish candor Hiram countered, "Surely when you look at her, Uncle, you can imagine how difficult such a promise would be to keep."

Matthias stepped very close to Hiram and ground out, "You will not touch her again."

Hiram's eyes hardened momentarily. Then he grinned and backed away. To Miriam he said cheerfully, "I see you have an escort home." He strode away, light on his feet for his size.

Miriam, still clinging to Matthias, cried, "You could have been hurt! You could have been arrested!" Her face crumpled.

"Come." Matthias drew her into a short alley that led to a sheltered courtyard. Out of the wind and away from the traffic, he drew her into his arms and held her close. Through the heavy folds of their two cloaks he could barely detect the shape of her body, but could feel her shaking. Independent Miriam was crying.

When she quieted, he continued to hold her, resting his chin on the top of her head. When she looked up, he kissed her as he had wanted to do for so long. A sense of oneness with her swept over him. Was there ever a time he had not loved her? This was what the Scriptures meant when they said a man must leave his mother and father and cling to his wife.

The word *wife* jolted him to reality. He was embracing her as a man embraces his wife. Reluctantly he held her at arm's length. "I wanted so to see you alone. Yet now I don't know what to say."

"What do you mean?" she demanded.

For a moment he wished she were like other women. She might be less inclined to question his decisions. He tried to explain. "I love you dearly. It troubles me not to be able to approach you honorably as a man who can care for a wife."

A puzzled frown furrowed her smooth brow. "I really don't understand why you can't marry and still keep your vow." This time her characteristic directness made it easier for him.

"Jesus has said if anyone puts father, mother, wife, or family ahead of him, that person is not worthy to be his disciple."

"How can he say such a thing—as if he were God!"

He could understand her hurt, but her anger against Jesus separated them as nothing else could. He let go of her. "Miriam, others might serve Jesus and a bride also, but I cannot. If you can't understand, perhaps I have wronged you by asking you to wait for me."

"Your love for me is so great that you put Jesus of Nazareth before me?" she scoffed. "And you will help him conquer Rome with love. Don't talk to me of such love. He may have healed your hand, but he has crippled your mind."

"If you really believe that, then we can never marry!"

"You are proving the truth of my words!" she flared back.

"Come," he said quietly. "I'll walk you home."

She said no more on the way, nor did he. At the cheese shop they parted without a word.

The next morning Joel's voice awakened Matthias.

"Joel! Where have you been? I searched the city for you."

"I've been staying in the lower city with friends. If I'd known you were here, I would have come sooner, but Matthias, I have terrible news. Herod has killed John the Baptist!"

Matthias sat up and threw off his covers. "John? Dead?"

"His disciples say the king beheaded him . . . and displayed his head on a platter at his banquet!" Joel grimaced.

"Oh no," groaned Matthias. "Have you told Shebuel?"

"No."

"Good. I'll go to him."

But Shebuel was up and already had heard of the tragedy.

"I must go tell Jesus," said Matthias.

The old man bowed his head. "I fear all the more for him and for you." His hands shook as he reached out for Matthias and clung to him briefly. "Go carefully, my son."

Returning to Joel, Matthias said, "Please watch over Shebuel. He's not as strong as he wants us to believe."

"I had planned to move from here. My life has changed since you were last in Jerusalem. I'm obligated to others." Joel hesitated, obviously withholding information.

"Joel, did Neriah have any just cause for saying you weren't acceptable for the academy?"

"None." Joel looked him in the eyes. He was telling the truth, but also declaring his independence.

Matthias smiled. "All right, as one friend to another, I ask you to stay here just until Shebuel grows stronger."

"If you think he needs me, I will work it out," Joel agreed.

Out in the streets Jerusalem quivered under the shock of Herod's debased execution of the prophet. People whispered the news of the Baptist's gory death. Some said Herod had fallen into a fit of rage after his drunken act and was on his way to the holy city. Above the temple the sacrificial smoke had billowed sideways and was falling back toward the hills in a blotchy haze, as if the heavens had rejected the offering.

A sense of impending doom crept over Matthias.

At the home above the cheese shop the women were weeping.

With outrage Cleopas demanded, "Why in the name of our father Abraham does God permit a vile person such as Herod to take the life of a true prophet? Herod's not fit to stand on the same soil as John the Baptist!"

"You answer your own question," said Matthias. "John no longer has to walk on an Earth defiled by Herod." Even as he spoke, the knot of pain in his own chest eased.

Hannah shook her head mournfully, but Miriam's face cleared. "I just told myself the same thing. Surely this righteous man is in the bosom of Abraham and is receiving his reward."

Cleopas cast his sister a respectful glance and admitted, "As the God of Israel lives, you're both right. Yet my hands cry to avenge the Baptist."

Hannah returned to a seat and brushed aimlessly at wool she had been carding. Cleopas dropped down beside her. Miriam snatched up the ever-present spinning she had laid aside and returned to her stool. Frowning, she dried her cheeks with the back of her hand and began to whirl the spindle.

Matthias, unable to settle in one place, paced the floor. "Jesus says no man born is greater than John. He says too that the happiest people are those who are persecuted for the sake of righteousness. The Kingdom of Heaven is theirs."

Miriam broke in with a tight voice, "Does he mean we must be mistreated like John in order to participate in the kingdom Jesus proclaims?"

"No. He says God's rewards and the joy of being with God outweigh anything we might suffer. I think Jesus means to give us courage and hope."

The lines between her brows deepened. "I don't even want to need courage and hope," she said angrily.

Cleopas glanced sympathetically at his sister deftly feeding wool toward the spindle. "Nor do any of us, Miriam. But it does help to remember God's rewards."

"It is as Rabbi Ebed says," Miriam replied passionately. "The Nazarene speaks with two tongues. For all his talk of love, he prepares his followers for violence." She continued rhythmically to spin, holding the distaff high. *Like a battle standard,* thought Matthias. *She is so determined to fight against the Master.* But the sight of her arrested him in midstride. In the colorless room she stood out like a vessel of burnished gold would shine in an ironsmith's shop. As though he'd spoken, she met his eyes and then looked away.

"Matthias," said Cleopas, "the Pharisees have been complaining that Jesus is gaining more of a following than John had. Now if they can influence Herod . . ."

"Herod will go after Jesus next," Matthias finished. "I'm going to warn him."

Miriam scrambled to her feet, ignoring the spindle that clattered to the floor. "But to go now invites Herod's attention!"

"The king has no eye for rug merchants," Matthias remarked dryly.

Both women turned to Cleopas. "Don't let him do this foolish thing," Hannah pleaded.

Cleopas hoisted himself to his feet, raised his hands, and shushed them as though they were children. "This is for Matthias to decide. None of us has the right to try to deter him. Jesus is not only his friend, but also his healer."

A frenzied pounding on the door interrupted them. Cleopas went, bent his ear to listen, and then opened the door cautiously.

Joel pushed in. "Is Matthias here? Matthias! You must flee the city! They're searching for you!"

"What? Who?"

"Soldiers led by Neriah. When they couldn't find you, Neriah ordered them to seize Shebuel."

"They'll kill him!" said Matthias. "I must go and seek his release."

"No. Wait!" Cleopas grabbed him. "Joel, did they say why they wanted Matthias?"

"I heard Neriah mention rebellion. While they searched for you, Shebuel signaled me to warn you. They haven't hurt him. It's you they want."

Matthias twisted free of Cleopas. "I can't leave with him in their hands."

"Think, Matthias," Cleopas argued. "Neriah is counting on that. And what chance will you have against him? Anything you say or do, he'll use against you—and Jesus."

"They have no grounds to hold Shebuel," added Joel. "He's an old man. If you don't appear, they'll let him go."

"Matthias, you must flee," urged Hannah.

"Oh, hurry, Matthias," Miriam pleaded. "If Neriah is in this, he'll think to come here. You must hurry!"

With a sinking sensation, Matthias realized they were right. Staying to fight for Shebuel's release could involve his whole family and might harm the cause of the Master.

Joel said, "I have friends who can get you out of the city, but you must come quickly."

Reluctantly Matthias agreed.

"Get him the poorest garment you can find, with enough to it to shield his face," Joel ordered, assuming command as naturally as if he'd always done so. "And something for me too, if you can." As he spoke he removed the good cloak he wore and handed it to Cleopas. Matthias did likewise.

The women left and soon returned with ragged, soiled clothes from the storeroom.

In a short time Joel transformed them both into dirty beggars with feet bare and faces begrimed with lampblack.

At last Matthias met Joel's new friends, a motley bunch who looked like beggars, but who, at Joel's arrival, began to act with military precision.

"Don't ask questions," warned Joel. "I'll explain later."

To Matthias's amazement, he was passed from one dark hovel to another along a dismal alley until the city gate loomed nearby. There he was pushed down against a lame man begging just within the gate. The man shouted at his intrusion and thrust him out into the traffic with surprisingly strong hands. Other beggars slapped him and shouted.

A guard turned and upon seeing him grunted, "Get along, old man. We've more than enough of your sort here." He too pushed Matthias onward into the flow of the people leaving the city.

As Matthias stumbled to freedom, a man gave him a final shove, but at the same time slipped a pair of sturdy sandals into his hand.

Matthias hid the footwear under his rags and hobbled on. When he felt it was safe to look back, he could see no trace of Joel.

Twelve

Incredibly, less than a month later, Matthias returned to Judea, sent back by Jesus. On the Mount of Olives he paused and looked down on the city from which he had fled. In spite of Jesus' assurance that he would be safe, the sight of the gleaming white-and-gold temple stirred in him a feeling of foreboding. More than the Roman puppet Herod, Matthias feared Caiaphas, who could turn the world upside down when he claimed to speak for God.

Iscariot understood the possibilities too, and had insisted that Matthias should go to his friend Lemuel if danger threatened, for Lemuel possessed the power of great wealth.

What was the power of any man compared to the power of the Son of God? Matthias shrugged as if to cast an unwelcome hand from his shoulder and strode down the Mount, across the Kidron, and into the lower city. Trusting Jesus' word that he could safely do so, he marched directly to Shebuel's house.

There he learned that Shebuel had been held under arrest until Reuben had managed to obtain his release. As for Joel, Shebuel said, "I haven't seen him since the day after Reuben brought me home."

"I must find him," said Matthias. "He and Reuben may be able to tell me what I need to know about Neriah."

"After you fled for your life, why did Jesus send you back?"

"He told me to come and be a son to you while he took the Twelve far to the north. He said his loss of disciples would be reported here, and his lack of support would lull his enemies, making it safe for me. Neriah poses no real threat without the support of the rulers."

"How did Jesus lose followers?" asked Shebuel in surprise.

Matthias told him how Jesus had fed five thousand by miraculously multiplying a boy's lunch and then had refused to be made a king by the excited crowd. Instead, he'd told them he was bread from heaven, and if they ate his body and drank his blood, they would have eternal life.

Unlike the disciples in Capernaum, Shebuel did not find the teaching impossible. As he listened his worry lines faded.

Later, while preparing for bed, Matthias wondered if he had accurately presented the Lord's teaching. He understood so little himself. A wave of loneliness swept over him. He longed to be back in Galilee with Jesus, instead of attending to Shebuel's needs. He threw himself on his couch and morosely watched the shadows dance at the whim of the lamps. "Oh, Lord," he whispered across the miles. "Like Peter, my heart cries, 'Bid me come to you.' Why did you send me away?"

From his memory Jesus answered. "Happy are the meek who submit their will to God."

The words stung his conscience. To obey the Son of God was to obey God. He had come because Jesus had sent him. His head rested easier on his pillow. At an early hour he awoke and snuffed the lamps and dozed again.

Then someone called, "Oh, hurry! It is the master, sir."

A hand shook Matthias. Startled, he awoke. "What is it?"

"Shebuel has been stricken again. Come quickly!" With trembling hands, the servant Daniel held out a robe.

Matthias threw it on and rushed down the corridor. In his sleeping chamber Shebuel lay propped up on cushions, struggling for breath. Zibiah sat beside him, weeping and holding his hand.

The physician Alexander murmured, "Do not overtax him."

Matthias dropped to his knees beside Zibiah's chair and gently grasped Shebuel's other hand. At his touch the prostrate man opened his eyes and smiled. "You . . ." he rasped weakly, "must follow . . ." he fought for breath, "Jesus." Perspiration beaded his face. Zibiah gently wiped it away.

"Yes. Yes, I will, sir."

Shebuel whispered, "His way . . . is life."

"Don't talk now, Father. Just rest."

Shebuel smiled and with a burst of strength gave Zibiah's hand to Matthias. To Zibiah he whispered, "My beloved," and to Matthias, "My . . . son!" His struggle for breath ceased. As they watched, the flame of life in his eyes dimmed and vanished.

Zibiah, recognizing the stare of death, fell across Shebuel, wailing. Refusing comfort, she clung to the body of her husband. The physician brought women servants, who knelt by their mistress and added their mourning cries to hers.

Numbly Matthias went to his room. His own grief was a stone in his chest. Tears had never come readily for him, and now his sorrow defied expression. He had done so little to show Shebuel how much he loved and honored him. With remorse Matthias remembered that his last waking thoughts had been spent wondering how soon he could leave his adopted father.

At dawn Matthias went to make the tomb ready. His mourning alienated him from the waking city. It incensed him that people should be starting the day as if it were any other day. He wanted to shout, "Shebuel ben Azariah, a righteous man, has died! Are good men so plentiful that we do not miss one?" Instead, he trudged silently to the burial place.

As always, Shebuel had prepared. Matthias found the tomb ready, with the stone propped in place. Standing inside the tiny burial chamber, Matthias recalled Shebuel's last words about Jesus. His adopted father had believed in the Master as truly as Matthias did. Little as Matthias could comprehend of eternal life, he felt a profound peace for Shebuel.

In the clarity of that peace came a surprising thought. Had the Master somehow known that Shebuel was about to die and intentionally sent Matthias with the message about eternal life? Foreknowledge of death was no more impossible than feeding a multitude with a boy's lunch. It would be so like the Master to take care of Shebuel, while at the same time easing Matthias's grief. At last Matthias wept.

Assuming ownership of the business presented no immediate problem to Matthias, but caring for Zibiah did. She grieved and grew weaker. Matthias stayed home with her for long periods. Although Hannah and Miriam came daily with gifts of food, Matthias didn't visit even the cheese shop. For Shebuel's sake, as well as Zibiah's, he would not leave her. Tobias could manage the rug shop alone, as he had for many months.

Finally one day, while Zibiah was sleeping, concern for Joel overwhelmed Matthias. His young friend hadn't heard about Shebuel's death or he would have come.

Matthias went to the city gate where he'd last seen Joel. With little effort he spied a familiar dirty face and motioned to the man. As he dropped a coin in the outstretched hand, he said quietly, "I seek Joel of the house of Aaron."

The man shot him a surprised glance and then bowed his head. "I know no one by that name," he muttered.

"You know me. The last time you saw me, you shoved me out this gate and put sandals in my hand."

The beggar's eyes flicked over his face again. With lips barely moving, he whispered, "Follow me at a distance. Where I enter an alley, you enter the door on its right." Aloud he whined, "The Lord bless you, most generous master."

Matthias obeyed instructions and found himself in a narrow shop filled with brass bells, harnesses, halters, and bridles.

A man with an oily smile greeted him. "You honor my humble shop, sir, but your expert eye judged rightly. I can provide you with the finest of bells and leather for a mere pittance."

"I see the quality of your merchandise, friend, but I didn't come to buy. I seek Joel of the house of Aaron. I am Matthias, son of Aaron, son of Shebuel."

"Matthias!" The man's manner changed instantly from ingratiating to dignified. "I will send for Joel. Come rest while you wait." He pulled Matthias through heavy curtains into a surprisingly large room filled with chairs and a table. The man waved him to a seat and hurried out.

Soon Joel rushed in. "Matthias! What are you doing here?"

"Jesus sent me back. Joel . . . Shebuel has died."

Joel collapsed onto a chair. "Only a few days ago my men reported he was growing stronger each day!" He shook his head with remorse. "I should have stayed with him . . . but I had to leave the city!" Then his face hardened. "Neriah killed him. Shebuel could have had many more comfortable years."

"He was old and ailing. I think his time had come."

"You didn't see how broken he was by the time Reuben obtained his release. They so dishonored him—the one who pulled me from the slave block and gave me life!" He dropped his face to his hands and shook with voiceless sobs.

Matthias waited for Joel's first grief to run its course. When the young man quieted, Matthias said, "Can you get a message to Reuben for me?"

"Yes. I reached him in time to save Shebuel from Neriah. Matthias, when Reuben walked in with orders for his release, they had stripped Shebuel of his clothes and were ready to whip him. Neriah stood there like Herod himself, giving the orders."

"How could he? I mean, by what authority?"

"By the high priest's authority and with men in temple guard uniforms. Of course Caiaphas denies that, and we've seen no trace of the guards since."

"How did Reuben prevail against such infamy?"

"He gathered men who knew Shebuel and masterfully presented his case to the Sanhedrin. Thank God for those who still honor the Law. The high priest didn't disagree with their judgment and claimed no knowledge of Neriah's high-handed breach of the Law, but he did intercede for Neriah to keep his position at the School of Hillel. Neriah suffered disgrace, but did not lose wealth or power."

"You are certain of all this?"

"I swear by the very throne of heaven. I have many eyes and ears in high places as well as low. But you've brought me news of my first failure. I must find out why my men didn't know about Shebuel's death."

"So it was Neriah all the way." Matthias's jaw tightened. "He has surpassed himself this time."

"He deserves death, but like many others in this city, he will continue to prosper and abuse any who step into his path."

The young man's bitterness grieved Matthias. This too was the result of Neriah's hand. "Joel, how have you come to this?" Matthias waved his hand at the military precision apparent in the room, and the disquieting glimpse of a dagger on the wall near each door.

"One day I saw Ismail, the man who owns this shop, and recognized him. He was my father's friend. Matthias, I'm a true-born Jew of the tribe of Benjamin. My father was a ruler in Seleucia. With Ismail's help I began to remember those days before robbers killed my father and mother.

"I spent all my free time with Ismail and began to help him when I saw how he succored many of the poor. Because of my education and because Ismail told people my father had been a ruler, they began to turn to me as their leader. I only helped them obtain honest work, but Neriah discovered my frequent visits and twisted the meaning." Anger flashed across Joel's expressive face. "When he cast me out of the academy, it was a short step to the stealth I now practice. I am dedicated to helping the helpless."

"But how do you accomplish this?"

"Some of my men have survived by their swift fingers and a few by the sword."

"You lead a band of thieves?" gasped Matthias.

"If need be. I myself work for Ismail and another shopkeeper, buying, selling, and keeping the accounts. We all use whatever talents we have to help widows and orphans and victims such as Shebuel." Joel held his head high. Nothing of the slave boy showed on his countenance. "Already I have led a slave to freedom—that's what took me from Jerusalem as soon as I knew Shebuel was home safely. And two other slaves who have escaped from abusive masters have found shelter with me."

"In the name of all that's holy, Joel, you could be condemned to slavery in the galleys for that!"

Joel's eyes turned flinty. "What I have chosen, I have chosen."

"But what future will you have?" demanded Matthias.

"My own. Just as you have yours, following Jesus."

Matthias could not but respect Joel's strength and courage. Seeing that he couldn't sway the young man from his course, Matthias said, "May the God of our fathers watch over you, Joel."

The young man's expression softened. "And you, Matthias."

Matthias cleared his throat. "I need to talk with Reuben. May I meet him here?"

Joel nodded. "I'll let you know when to come."

At the doorway to the shop, they parted. Joel cautioned, "Take care. Remember, Neriah has not had his fangs removed."

With the tasks of the rug shop and seeing to Zibiah's needs, each passing day made Jesus seem further away. By the time Matthias received word to come meet with Reuben, the months with the Master seemed like another lifetime.

On the way to Ismail's shop, each shabby beggar Matthias passed reminded him of Joel's dangerous activity. In this city where Romans oppressed Jews, and Jews oppressed Jews, Joel wouldn't have a hair of a chance for mercy if he were caught.

At the appointed hour Matthias entered the little bell and leather shop, and Ismail ushered him quickly to the back room.

Reuben, attired more simply than usual, rose from his chair and embraced Matthias. "I didn't know of Shebuel's death until he was buried. Then it seemed wiser to stay away from you."

Matthias followed Reuben back to his chair at the table and sat across from him. "Joel says Neriah ordered Shebuel seized and was even preparing to have him whipped."

Reuben nodded. "He somehow acquired an armed guard. Caiaphas denied any part in it, but I don't believe Neriah could have done it without him. I never thought Neriah could commit such injustice. I apologize for all the times I accused you of having a stinging nose when there was no smoke."

Matthias shook his head and waved his hand. "Forget it. I wish you had been right about Neriah and I wrong. Not only has he destroyed Shebuel and Zibiah, but Joel may be next. Joel's bitterness is bending him toward an ill fate. Shebuel's heart would break to see him now."

"Can't you get him to leave this and work in the rug shop?"

Matthias sighed. "Perhaps in time . . . if he lives long enough. Has he told you that his real father was a ruler?"

"No. Only that he was a Jew."

"I know little more than that, but knowing about his father has filled him with new confidence. And right now he's fueled by outrage. I can only hope he will listen to the teachings of Jesus. I wish I could persuade him to go with me when I return to Galilee."

"You will return, then?"

"Yes, after Passover, if I can leave Zibiah." He sounded more sure than he felt. The tentacles of daily responsibilities held him fast. He couldn't think beyond today and the hurt Neriah had wrought in the lives of innocent people. "What is Neriah doing now?" he asked abruptly.

Reuben leaned his elbows heavily on the table. "He no longer speaks to me, but treats Father with respect. He still keeps Elizabeth confined to her home. I haven't seen her since I sought Shebuel's release."

"May God do unto him all that he deserves," Matthias muttered. "And may I have a part in it."

For the first time in Matthias's memory, Reuben didn't try to dissuade him from his wish for vengeance.

Thirteen

At the rug shop neither the work nor the passage of time cooled Matthias's temper. Joel had been right. Neriah had brought Shebuel to a premature death. Moreover, he had driven Joel into intrigues that could put him back into slavery—or worse.

Matthias attacked the cords around a heap of bound rugs.

"Matthias!" Hannah's voice rang from the front of the shop.

He dropped his knife, glad for the interruption, and went to meet her. Miriam and the two boys were with her.

"You're a welcome sight," he said. "Come and rest awhile."

The children ran to watch Tobias hang the finest of the new rugs while Matthias and the women retired to what had been Shebuel's semiprivate room in the back of the shop. Laying aside their baskets, the women sank gratefully into the plush cushions. Matthias drew up a stool.

"Is there anything we can do for Zibiah?" asked Hannah.

"Now that she's up, perhaps she would welcome brief visits."

"We'll do that," said Miriam. Then abruptly she asked, "Have you any news from Jesus?"

"No. Nor have I expected any. He journeyed north to stay out of Herod's sight."

"So he finally fears Herod?" Hannah asked anxiously.

"He fears no man," Matthias replied.

"Well, fleeing isn't exactly fearless behavior," Miriam remarked.

"He goes because it is God's will. He is teaching the Apostles and preaching to people who haven't yet heard him."

Miriam's green eyes studied him. "You surely can't leave Zibiah now to follow Jesus."

"No, at least not until the Master returns from the north."

"Perhaps he will not return. Perhaps among the Gentiles, with their many gods, he will find a home," she exclaimed, her voice brittle with animosity.

"Miriam," cried Hannah, "Jesus is a righteous Jew!"

"He is a blasphemer and a sorcerer, just as Rabbi Ebed has always said."

"You can't mean that," Matthias protested. "You don't know what you're saying."

Eyeing him squarely, she said, "You know that's not true. I know exactly what I am saying."

Yes, with her uncommon knowledge of the Law, she knew the full penalty for blasphemy and sorcery. Torn by hearing the woman he loved denounce the man for whom he would die, Matthias leaned over and caught her wrist with his healed hand. "What of this?" he demanded, raising her imprisoned hand and shaking it.

"Such 'power' can come from Satan," she said coldly. "Jesus breaks the Law, yet claims he speaks for God. He twists the truth to his own ends, and I've watched him make a fool of you."

Matthias, who had never touched his sisters to discipline them, felt an intense urge to shake some sense into her. He dropped her hand and stood up. "I cannot entertain anyone who slanders my Master."

Her eyes blazed. Leaping to her feet, she rushed through the shop toward the street. In flight she looked so fragile and wounded, Matthias wanted to run after her and comfort her.

"Hurry and tell her you didn't mean it," Hannah urged.

"I can't," he said slowly. "I did mean it. If she believes what she said, there can be nothing between us. I know that Jesus is from God."

That night, without warning, Zibiah died quietly in her sleep. Matthias reopened Shebuel's tomb and buried her. After the mourners left, he lingered alone at the closed tomb. Cleopas had asked him to come home with them, but Matthias couldn't face Miriam. She had mourned Zibiah's death without even looking at him. And he had made no effort to bridge the gulf between them.

The sun's heat radiated from the stone that sealed the sepulcher, but Matthias felt the same sense of peace that had come to him the day he'd prepared it for Shebuel's burial. "Jesus knew you needed me," he whispered in farewell. "And now together may you enjoy the rest of the righteous."

He turned to leave and in midstride froze, his senses assaulted by the intrusion of Roman law. On the crest of the Hill of the Skull stood two crosses holding the agonized bodies of men trapped between life and death. While carrying Zibiah's bier he hadn't noticed them. Since the mass execution of most of the men of Sepphoris when he was ten, the sight of crucifixion twisted his belly. He swallowed hard, gathered the front of his robe in a tight fist, and hurried into the city.

After Zibiah's funeral, indecision hobbled Matthias. He could return to Capernaum, leaving the house and shop in Tobias's able hands. Or he could stay in the holy city until after Passover, as Jesus had suggested. Finally Matthias realized he didn't want to leave without trying to make peace with Miriam. So he invited her whole family to dinner, hoping she could not escape coming.

He succeeded. She came. Ethan's booming voice and the boys' laughter brought life to the big house. As they dined Ethan kept everyone laughing at his stories.

Finally Joseph squirmed at his mother's side. "Grandfather, when will you play 'Thieves' with us?"

"We must wait for torchlight, as Hiram taught you."

Cleopas remarked, "I wish Hiram had not introduced them to that street game. They are too young to separate fact from pretend."

"It didn't harm you, Son, nor will it harm them. That reminds me, Miriam, when is it Hiram is to dine with us?"

"The first day of the week." She reached for her wine goblet, and, finding it empty, set it back down.

Matthias poured for her. "So you've decided to be friends with Hiram?" he asked.

"He's never been an enemy," she said levelly.

In the silence that fell between them, David said, "Grandfather, I see them lighting the torches."

Ethan hoisted himself to his feet. "Matthias, this has been a feast. Now I beg your leave. As you see, I am needed in the garden."

Matthias stood. "Of course, sir."

"Wife, let's watch," Cleopas remarked. "I'll warrant you never had such a game in Nazareth."

Miriam arose to follow the rest of the family.

"I've been wanting to talk to you, Miriam," Matthias pleaded.

"Why?" she asked without turning.

"To ask you to forgive me for my rude behavior in the shop the other day."

For a moment he thought she would reject his plea. Then she faced him and said, "You're the first man I've ever heard admit to a fault, let alone ask forgiveness. I scarcely know what to say."

"Say you forgive me."

With eyes downcast, she said simply, "I do."

"Good!" he exclaimed, marveling at how much happiness two words could bring. In the hope of pleasing her, he said, "Come, I have something to show you!"

He took her to the chest of treasured scrolls in what had been Shebuel's favorite room. Lifting out the oldest, he unwrapped it and laid it on top of the chest for her to read. They knelt together, following the ancient language with Shebuel's silver pointer. Miriam could read Aramaic, Latin, and Greek, but was still learning Hebrew. Matthias was amazed at her quick grasp of new words. Too bad, he thought, that she hadn't been born a man.

He caught himself in midthought. Miriam a man? What an absurd idea. While she studied the Law, he studied her—her soft hair, her eyes hidden behind her dark lashes, her lips tenderly curved. She looked up. He was closer than was proper, but she didn't move away. Keeping his hands at his sides, he leaned forward and kissed her lips . . . gently at first, and then urgently, when he felt her eager response. When he drew back from her, he saw tears spilling down her cheeks.

"Miriam, don't cry!" he exclaimed.

"Oh, Matthias, I've been so miserable thinking you despised me. Don't ever send me away again." She threw herself at him, wrapped her arms around his neck, and pressed her wet cheek against his.

Caught off balance, he fell backward with her on top. They collapsed in laughter.

Matthias gasped, "Miriam, get up before someone sees us."

"If you promise to be friends forever," she teased.

"I'll promise anything. Only get up."

"Anything?" she asked seriously.

"No."

Their light mood vanished.

She stood, and then he. He kept his distance while she stared up at him expectantly.

"Little Miriam. How you have grown," he murmured.

She smiled slowly. "I used to wonder if you'd ever notice."

He hesitated. He could guide the conversation into impersonal channels, or he could say what she wanted to hear. He submitted to the inevitable. "I've known you were a woman for a long time, Miriam."

"How long?" she challenged, her smile growing.

"Since the time we went to hear John the Baptist preach."

She sobered and said softly, "I thought you looked at me without seeing."

"Sometimes a man dares not let a woman know what he sees."

"Why, Matthias?" she cried.

He winced at the hurt in her voice. Desperately wanting her to understand, he began, "During the years I cared for my family, I learned to ignore my own interests and desires."

She nodded, her expression tender with sympathy.

She had to know it all. He continued stiffly, "There was a young woman I loved. I couldn't marry her, but for a long time I couldn't forget her." He met her startled eyes and hurried on. "That's all in the past. Please believe that when I look at you, it's as if she never existed." He caught her hands and held them against his breast. "Miriam, one more thing I beg you to understand. Truly I must follow Jesus, and I don't know where he will lead."

She pressed her forehead against their clasped hands and asked shakily, "Are you saying you don't want me?"

He gathered her close in his arms. With his cheek against her hair, he whispered, "Oh, Miriam, sweet Miriam. How could I not want you?" Then he gently held her at arm's length, where he could see her face. Her arm, firm and warm under his fingers, made him acutely aware of his two strong hands. Even this pleasure of loving touch he owed to Jesus. Suddenly it was as if Jesus himself were standing there with them. Matthias relaxed his hold on Miriam.

She stiffened, as if she also sensed the presence of the person in his thoughts.

"Miriam, try to understand," Matthias pleaded. "For me, Jesus must come first."

She bowed her head and shook it in denial. "I'm so frightened for you! I'm so glad you've been healed, but I can't ignore what Rabbi Ebed says. Jesus has broken the Law. I don't understand how you can follow him, yet you say he must come first! Next to God, a man's family should come first. It is God's will that a man should marry and have children."

Matthias let his hands fall at his sides. "Let there be honesty between us always. I can never live as other men without following Jesus first."

She gave him an anguished look. Tears sprang to her eyes.

His careful control cracked. Snatching her to him, he held her close. "Don't weep, my love. God forgive me if this breaks my covenant, but can't we give ourselves time to see if it be right for us to marry?"

"Yes," she agreed. "Oh yes, Matthias." She melted against him and pulled his head down to kiss him. Her lips on his sealed their private betrothal.

While Matthias's future remained unsettled, he couldn't talk to Ethan. Neither did he dare to single out Miriam from the rest of the family when he visited. And the more he saw her, the more he wanted to forsake his vow and ignore her opposition to Jesus. Finally he decided that staying near her was a mistake. When he told the family he would return to Galilee on the morrow, Miriam turned cool and distant.

Lonely and hurt, Matthias went to Ismail's shop, praying that Joel would not also disappoint him.

But in the secret meeting room, Joel's face clouded over when Matthias urged him to accompany him to Capernaum.

"Last summer I would have come, but not now. My life is here. I've set my course and it doesn't lead to Galilee."

"You don't know where it will lead," argued Matthias.

"Do you know where Jesus leads?"

Joel sat at the rude table as erect as a soldier. Matthias read his own defeat in the boy's eyes, but persisted. "Because I know him, I can trust my course to him."

"That's not enough for me. Here, I am giving some people a chance for freedom." He leaned forward on his elbows. "I've made a way to take slaves beyond the eastern borders of Rome."

"And who will rescue you when you're caught?"

Joel shrugged. "If God is merciful, I shall not be caught."

Matthias sighed and stood up. He wished he could return to the days when he could command and Joel would obey. No. The boy had grown as strong as Matthias had wished. He held out his hand. "May God's mercy rain down on you, Joel. And may you ever follow the light of his Word."

The next morning when Matthias went to say good-bye to his family, Miriam kept Hannah between herself and him. He could not even touch her hand without pursuing her. Hurt, and then irritated, he stamped down the stairs with everyone's farewell but Miriam's ringing in his ears.

At the bottom he glanced back. Miriam now stood in front of them all, her hand raised in a hesitant salute. "May God go with you, Matthias," she called in an unsteady voice.

"And with you," he responded, his hurt melting under the warmth of the love in her voice. No wonder she couldn't understand his need to leave her. At this moment of parting, neither could he.

Fourteen

When Matthias at last rejoined the Master and the Apostles, his joy was short-lived. While on Mt. Hermon, Jesus had predicted his death at the hands of evil men.

No one had dared to question him after he'd severely rebuked Peter for declaring that Jesus must not die. So the Twelve decided among themselves that no one had power as great as the Master, and therefore he must be speaking symbolically.

Matthias, like the others, refrained from asking him about his frightening teaching. Unlike the others, Matthias worried that somehow it might be foreknowledge. Hadn't Jesus known about Shebuel's impending death? Or was that, after all, a coincidence?

Maybe I dread talk of death because I've seen so much of it recently. And because Joel has chosen to live in its shadow.

Harvest time brought the wealth of the land to Capernaum's tree-lined streets. Melons, apricots, grapes, eggplants, cucumbers, and figs brightened vendor's stalls. Blended with the sweet perfume of fruits, the pungent odors of garlic and leeks drifted on the hot summer breeze.

Jesus talked no more of death, but of the coming Kingdom. By the end of summer, when Jesus decided to attend the Feast of Tabernacles, Matthias had lost his anxiety. He'd seen too many miracles to believe anyone could harm Jesus. And true to his expectation, in Jerusalem no one hindered Jesus. In the temple Pharisees argued viciously against him and temple guards seemed about to seize him, but Jesus simply walked away through crowds that made way for him.

When Jesus finally went to Bethany, Matthias hurried to see Miriam and found the family changed. Hannah was expecting another child. She rested a hand on her rounded belly and smiled contentedly. "God has honored our prayers. This babe will be born near your birth time, Matthias."

"Yes," said Cleopas. "Before Passover we can take him to the temple for dedication."

"Him?" Matthias laughed.

"This family can't imagine a daughter," broke in Miriam. "It's good to see you, Matthias."

"And you," he answered. *How have I lived without you these long months?* he thought. Aloud he said, "Jesus went to Bethany as usual, but I wanted to be here . . ."

Cleopas, unmindful of the unspoken messages passing between Matthias and Miriam, asked, "What brings Jesus to Jerusalem now, after missing Passover? Do you think it's safe?"

"Well, this afternoon people listened to him more eagerly than ever. Even the temple guards gave ear. Soon all Israel shall see the power of Jesus."

"You talk like a soldier," said Miriam in quick disapproval. "And I can't imagine temple guards—such as Hiram—listening with any sympathy to the Nazarene."

"I never saw Hiram." He kept his voice cool, but the very name irritated him.

"Well, you'll see him soon," said Hannah. "He's joining us for supper. You'll stay, won't you?"

Disappointment made him abrupt. "No. I wish to see Joel yet tonight."

All the way to Ismail's shop, he wished he had stayed. Even with Hiram there, at least he could have been near Miriam.

When he reached the small shop, however, thoughts of Miriam fled. The shop was nailed shut and sealed with the mark of Rome. Matthias stared, unable to take it in.

He paced the width of the shop, trying to see through cracks in the barricade, as though Joel could be hidden in some dark cranny. Frantic, he peered up and down the darkening street. The few people he'd seen had disappeared, all but one old woman who pecked her way along with a stick. He hurried to her.

"Shalom," he said. "Can you tell me of Ismail?" He gestured at the boarded-up shop.

Fear pinched her wizened face. "No, I know nothing." She bent her head and advanced her cane, trying to evade him.

He restrained her with a quick hand. "But you must have seen or heard something. How long ago did this happen?"

"Let me go!" Her voice rose in terror. "I know nothing!"

He released her, and as an act of contrition felt in his pouch for a coin. Pressing it into her rough hand, he said, "I didn't mean to frighten you, Old Mother."

Her fingers clamped tightly around the coin. "I saw nothing," she whimpered and tottered away.

Oh, God, where is Joel?

Matthias knocked on nearby doors, but no one answered. He hurried to the city gate to look for a familiar beggar. Only guards and gatekeepers were there. They eyed him suspiciously.

In desperation he turned up the hill toward the house of ben Joed.

Reuben drew him into the small guest room just inside the gate. He said, "Only yesterday I learned that Ismail's shop was closed, and no one would tell me anything. The men Joel organized may have fled to the caves in the hills."

"Could he have escaped with them?"

Reuben's face registered the answer. "Today, through Father's friends, I learned he was flogged and cast into prison. They say he was hiding a favored slave from the household of Pontius Pilate. You saw the Roman seal on the shop door. If he survives flogging, they'll send him to the galleys."

Matthias suppressed a shudder. He wanted to roar no . . . no! Past the tightness in his throat, he choked, "I begged him to come to Galilee with me, but he wouldn't listen."

"You did what you could. A man must do what a man must do."

"That's what Joel said."

"He learned it from you."

"Why could he not have learned from my mistakes?"

"For the same reason none of us learns that way."

"Reuben, is Joel's arrest more of Neriah's work?"

Reuben sighed. "I wish I could assure you it wasn't. I will try to find out."

"Joel is like my own son. I'd do anything to ransom him."

They parted on Reuben's promise, "I'll do all I can."

After a sleepless night, Matthias trudged to the Pool of Siloam to meet Jesus. Even Jesus could not help Joel, unless he declared himself Messiah.

Matthias kept remembering the thin, frightened face of the slave boy Shebuel had brought to him during the first year he had worked for the rug merchant. Joel had suffered abuse that would have maddened many adults, yet had grown into a man of compassion.

Oh, God, how much longer must we suffer? How much more Israelite blood must be spilled? If Jesus were king . . .

Matthias's grief isolated him from the festal crowd. He couldn't think of anything but Joel beaten and perhaps dying in a filthy dungeon—within walking distance, yet as far from Matthias's help as if he were in Rome.

During the procession to the temple and the ritual there, Matthias participated from habit. He was barely aware of anything until suddenly after the pouring of the water on the altar, Jesus shouted, "If any man thirst, let him come to me and drink! He who believes on me, as Scripture has said, shall pour forth rivers of living water!"

Matthias jumped, as startled as everyone else. Jesus spoke of the Scripture that foretold the great outpouring of God's Spirit at the coming of God's Kingdom. Coming as it did after the symbolic outpouring of God's Spirit—the pouring of the water on the altar—his proclamation should show them the Master was the long-awaited Anointed One.

People on all sides murmured, some astonished, some approving, and some protesting.

Oh, God, let him say he is our Messiah. Let it be in time to save Joel.

To Matthias's sorrow, Jesus said nothing more. The sacrifice proceeded as though the Nazarene had never spoken.

The next day, with no word from Reuben regarding Joel, Matthias stayed with Jesus while he taught in the temple. Again the people heard him gladly. But the scribes and Pharisees shouted, "Your testimony means nothing. A man cannot lawfully bear witness about himself."

Jesus replied, "My witness is true. I and the Father who sent me bear witness together."

Matthias spied temple guards approaching, circling the crowd warily. He nudged Andrew and nodded toward them. The big man tensed and whispered to Peter.

Word passed quickly from one disciple to the other, while Jesus continued, "I am going away. Where I am going, you cannot come."

Beside Matthias a stalwart Judean puzzled, "Is he saying he will kill himself? Where else could we not follow?"

"Stop talking of death," hissed Matthias.

The man glowered, but closed his mouth.

Jesus said, "I am not of this world. If you do not believe that I am the One from above, you will die in your sins."

The Pharisees grew angrier. They began to turn some of the people against Jesus.

Oh God, how can this be? Matthias braced himself for trouble and scanned the crowd. As he did so, his eyes met Neriah's. A bolt of anger flashed to the tips of Matthias's fingers, leaving them alive and ready for battle. The Pharisee stood a few paces away, his arms folded, his face as eager as that of a hungry carnivore. A cold smile stretched his lips. He was flanked by two temple guards.

Matthias clenched his fists, but could do nothing beyond keeping his eye on Neriah and the guards.

Jesus was saying, "If God were your father, you would love me, for he sent me to you. You can't even understand what I say, because your father is the devil."

Pure malice flooded Neriah's countenance.

"You are a Samaritan and have a devil yourself," shouted one of the guards, moving away from Neriah. Both of the guards left Neriah to join other guards, who had spread out among the people to surround the place where Jesus stood.

"I have no devil," Jesus countered. "I honor my Father. Truly, if a man keeps my word, he shall not taste death!"

"Now we know you have a devil!" yelled Neriah. "Abraham is dead and the prophets are dead. Are you greater than they?"

The guards pressed closer.

Jesus said, "My Father, whom you call your God, glorifies me."

"What did he say?" called one.

"He says our God is his Father!" spat another.

"Quiet! Let his lies condemn him!"

Jesus' words fell like the clean blow of a hammer on an anvil. "I know God and obey him. Abraham rejoiced to see me."

Neriah bellowed, "You are not yet fifty years old and you tell us you've seen Abraham?" His eyes glittered for the strike.

Jesus faced Neriah, and their gaze held until Neriah faltered and blinked.

"Truly, truly," thundered the Master, "before Abraham was, I Am!" He raised his arms high, palms upward, in a gesture of both proclamation and invitation.

Every sound ceased.

To hear Jesus speak the Unspeakable Name of God shocked even Matthias. Then the crowd exploded. Neriah's face contorted with rage. Raising his fist, he signaled the guards, but they were hindered by the surge of people.

"He blasphemes! Stone him!"

From a stonemason's work pile they snatched up jagged rocks and hurled them at Jesus. One thudded against Matthias's shoulder. He raised his arms to protect his head and tried to place himself between the attackers and Jesus.

It could not be, yet death closed in from all sides.

Fifteen

Jesus grabbed Matthias and shoved him and the others toward the nearest gate into the city. The Master kept his own body between the attackers and his disciples.

In utter confusion people let them pass, and then closed ranks behind them. There was no explaining it, but one moment they faced death, and the next they were free on the Xystos Bridge.

"Lord, they would have killed us," Matthias stammered.

"No," Jesus answered. "You shall not be harmed." The incredibility of their escape lent power to his words.

Nevertheless, Jesus retired to Bethany. Matthias accompanied him to the city gate, but he couldn't leave Jerusalem without knowing Joel's fate. And he wanted to reassure his family if they had heard of the attack on Jesus.

Ethan and Cleopas, busy with customers, saluted and motioned him upstairs. At the apartment door Matthias caressed the mezuzah and closed his eyes. *Oh God, have mercy on us all and protect this home.*

When he opened his eyes, Miriam stood waiting. From her expression he could tell she had heard nothing of the stoning. Hannah and Tamara were nowhere to be seen, but the children were chattering with Hannah in a distant sleeping room.

"Miriam." He opened his arms and she walked into them. Then children's voices warned them to part.

Hannah, heavy on her feet, waddled into the family room and shooed the boys out to play. "Matthias, I thought you'd be with Jesus!" she exclaimed.

"I was. Now he has gone to Bethany."

"So early?"

"Yes . . . we may be leaving for Galilee soon."

"But why?" asked Miriam. "The feast is not over."

"There was trouble. The Pharisees roused the people against Jesus."

"Oh no!" gasped Hannah.

"What did Jesus do to anger them this time?" cried Miriam.

"He claimed his father as witness to the truth of his words. Then they asked where his father was," said Matthias.

"What did he say?" asked Hannah eagerly.

"He said he came from God—that God was his father." Matthias turned to Miriam. "He spoke the Unspeakable Name as if it were his own."

Miriam paled. "Blasphemy! They will stone him!"

Hannah's face blanched. She staggered to a chair and collapsed onto it. Miriam hurried to her, slipped her arm around her shoulders, and pressed her hand against Hannah's forehead. "Get Cleopas!" she cried.

Matthias obeyed. Cleopas was at Hannah's side in a few moments. "Let me take you to lie down," he said, stooping to lift her.

"No. Please." She took a few deep breaths. "I'm fine now that I'm seated. I want to hear what happened to Jesus in the temple."

Cleopas straightened and stood beside her, keeping a protective hand on her shoulder. "What does she mean?" he asked.

Matthias told him what Jesus had said.

Cleopas's expression went from grave to shocked. "You could all have been killed! How did you escape?"

"Jesus pushed us out of the temple. No one hindered him. And no one followed. It was as if God himself intervened."

"You mean you just walked away?" asked Cleopas.

Matthias nodded. "When we got out into the street, Jesus told me no one could harm us."

"That's ridiculous! He's surely possessed!" cried Miriam.

"No," Matthias corrected, "he speaks for God. When he used the Name none of us dare pronounce with our unclean lips, it was as if the Most High were standing there before us. The Name was in him and on him and around him. I wanted to look away for fear . . . I would be gazing at the face of God."

Cleopas and Hannah stared at him, open-mouthed.

Miriam touched his arm with a trembling hand. "Oh, Matthias, please leave him before it's too late."

From the doorway Reuben cut off Matthias's reply. "Shalom," he said. "Ethan sent me up." His haggard appearance forewarned Matthias. "I bring bad news, my brother. Would you rather talk in private?"

Matthias beckoned him in. "Not unless . . . Cleopas?"

"We'll stay," said Cleopas.

"I found Joel," Reuben said. He lips twisted with pain. "I've obtained permission to bury him."

"Oh, God," Matthias whispered. "Oh, God, I would gladly have died for him."

Hannah began to wail, but Miriam quietly said to Reuben, "Bring his body here. Tamara will prepare it for burial."

When they brought the bruised, torn flesh that had been Joel, Matthias sat beside it, rocking as if in prayer, but he couldn't pray. Everything in him cried out against the injustice and cruelty that had devoured Joel. Everything in him cried out against his own impotence.

Finally he relinquished his vigil and Tamara set about the hard work of cleansing and wrapping the ravaged remains, and before sunset they buried him near the tomb of Shebuel.

"Stay with us tonight, Brother," urged Hannah.

To please her he agreed, but he longed to flee to Jesus.

The next morning, when the merciful forgetfulness of sleep faded, Matthias rose and from habit fulfilled the ritual of morning prayer. Though his body bowed down, his soul cried out against both life and death.

When he found Miriam alone in the main room, he said, "Come with me to a place alone. We must talk."

She followed him meekly down the outer stairs to the alley, where he stopped and faced her. "I failed Joel. I cannot also wrong you."

"What do you mean? You did your best for Joel. And how would you wrong me?"

"Except for me, Joel would be alive and perhaps still a student at the academy. And if Neriah should see you as an object of my love, he'd find a way . . ."

"You think Neriah led Pilate's men to Joel?"

"I'm sure of it. And even if he didn't, he cast the boy from the school and set him on this way that has led to death."

"Joel was no longer a boy," Miriam argued gently. "He chose his own course."

"Nevertheless, Neriah will stop at nothing to hurt me and to get at Jesus."

"You think he would harm me?"

"He will murder. I saw it in his eyes yesterday. And Joel's broken body confirms it." He started to take her hand, but stopped himself. "You must forget me and our pledge." His voice came out harsher than he intended. "I won't be coming here again . . . for a long time."

"Matthias, go if you must, but don't reject me! I'll wait for you . . . as long as you need." She tried to throw herself on him, but he caught her arms and held her off.

"I can't be your shield and provider. You must accept this," he demanded, clinging to his anger, lest her pain take him captive. He pushed her away. "I won't involve you in my portion, whatever it is."

"But you said Jesus promised no harm would come to you."

"So I believe. But I have only to recall Joel's suffering to realize I don't know what may happen. I do know Jesus made no promise to protect you from the likes of Neriah."

"Neriah! I'm tired of hearing his name! Has he turned your knees to water? He's only one man, and a little man at that," she said with contempt.

"Enough. With the death of Joel, Neriah has set my destiny and his. If there is any purpose for me, or any atonement, it is in serving Jesus. For this cause, I relinquish marriage and family."

"Matthias, I love you!"

Her cry stabbed like a sword thrust, yet he resisted her with a cold will he could not have mustered before Joel's death. "Good-bye, Miriam."

He would have had to harden himself against more pleas, but Cleopas called from above. "There you are! Reuben is here."

Miriam slumped against the wall. Matthias avoided her pleading eyes and went upstairs. He didn't look back and she didn't follow him.

Only Cleopas and Reuben awaited him in the upper room. Reuben, looking like he'd had little sleep, gripped Matthias's hand and said, "Neriah told me orders have been issued for the arrest of Jesus."

The news neither startled nor worried Matthias. "No one can arrest Jesus," Matthias explained patiently, as if talking to a young child.

Cleopas stepped closer. "How can you say that after seeing what they did to Joel?"

"Jesus is not a defenseless youth."

"But Matthias . . ." Cleopas sputtered.

Reuben sighed heavily. "I also found out that Neriah did direct Pilate's men to Joel. He had men spying and reporting on Joel from the day he left the academy."

"I knew it had to be," said Matthias. "That's why I was just leaving. No house is safe that succors me."

Unlike Miriam, they didn't argue.

Heedless of traffic, Matthias stalked down the city street. At the congested gateway he glanced back the way he'd come. A man a head taller than everyone else caught his eye. Hiram, without his temple guard uniform, stared back at him and instantly looked away, pretending not to see him.

Matthias stepped aside for an incoming caravan and leaned against a wall to watch Hiram. With studied indifference the man made his way out of the city and south along the Kidron Valley.

After the guard had disappeared, Matthias left the city, taking care to keep a loaded cart between himself and the southbound road. Once across the Kidron, he hastened toward Bethany, certain that Hiram had not witnessed his departure. Up the long slope of the Mount of Olives he trudged with only his grief to keep him company. Nothing could bring back Joel or his dream of marrying Miriam. Even if she believed in Jesus, all Matthias bar Aaron could offer a wife was danger and desertion.

When his hand had been healed, he hadn't been able to imagine wanting more, but now, without Miriam, he felt more maimed than ever.

Oh God, Jesus said you would bless me with far more than physical healing. Please grant me that greater gift.

Sixteen

Days later, in the hills of Judea, Matthias rose one morning, stretched in the autumn sunlight, and felt life returning to his grief-deadened limbs. That very morning Jesus called the disciples together and chose seventy men to go out by twos to preach and heal in his name.

Matthias was one of the Seventy. And Judas Iscariot chose him for his traveling partner. Matthias paced himself to the shorter man's stride, hoping that by the time they returned he'd better understand this likable, but unpredictable, Apostle.

Within an hour they came to a small village—a cluster of humble houses that looked as if they'd grown up, stone upon stone, from the hilltop. A bevy of children ran out to meet them, led by a barking, scruffy dog. Matthias gripped his walking stick firmly, ready to defend himself, but Judas knelt and coaxed it into tail-wagging friendliness.

A boy, not yet waist high, stopped a few feet from them.

"Shalom," Matthias offered.

"Shalom." His brown eyes almost filled his face.

Judas straightened from petting the dog and asked, "May we meet your father?"

"My father is dead." The boy blinked and stirred the thin soil with his toe. "Would you like to meet my grandfather?"

"Yes, we would," Judas replied.

The rest of the children surrounded them. "Why do you want to meet David's grandfather?" said one. "He can't visit like my grandfather. He can't hear anything you say!"

"All the more reason for us to meet him," said Matthias. "Will you take us to him, David?"

The boy led them to an old man, who sat soaking up the warmth of the sun at the side of a shabby little hut. Only after David touched his grandfather did the old man realize he had company. He arose stiffly and bowed. "Shalom," he said in a loud voice, mouthing the word carefully.

Judas took his hand and shouted, "In the name of Jesus of Nazareth, shalom!"

The man jumped as if he had been hit. He pulled away from Judas and clapped his hands over his ears. "Da-vid?"

"Yes, Grandfather?"

The man dropped to his knees, gripped his grandson by the shoulders, and cried, "I . . . can . . . hear you! I can hear!" He hugged the child to himself and rocked back and forth.

David laughed and patted his grandfather's wet cheek.

Matthias asked Judas, "What did you do? Did you pray?"

Iscariot's face registered as much surprise as the grandfather's. "You heard me. I did nothing but speak in Jesus' name. This is not the way it happened in Galilee. There we anointed people with oil and prayed."

Soon everyone in the village came to see what had happened to Zimri. Both Matthias and Judas healed several who were ill with the fevers of the cool season. Then they told the people about the Kingdom of God. When the sun slipped behind threatening clouds, David's grandfather, who now moved like a younger man, begged them to lodge with him.

Matthias said, "We would be honored, sir."

In the little house with its dirt floor and few sticks of furniture, they rested while the grandfather fanned charcoal to a warm glow.

From outside a voice called, "Shalom! David, are you there?"

"Eshtol," cried David, "come see Grandfather! He can hear me!"

A youth of about fifteen appeared. He hobbled in, leaning on a stout stick, his useless foot swathed in rags. "I heard. I left Orphah with the sheep as soon as I heard."

Eshtol knelt on the mat beside the older man. "Grandfather Zimri . . . can you really hear me?"

"I hear you well. You hurt my ears!" Laughing, he pressed his palms to his ears. "So much I hear! These men have healed me and others and tell us of a Nazarene who announces the coming of God's Kingdom."

"The Kingdom? Then Rome will be banished?"

"Yes, the Messiah will rule us at last!" Zimri exclaimed. "God sends the blessing of healing before his Anointed One."

The youth turned to Matthias. "This is true? The Messiah comes soon?"

"Yes. God sends these healings as a sign."

Hope flickered in the boy's eyes and then faded. He bowed his head. "I was born this way, but . . ." he faltered.

"Let me see your foot," said Matthias. The boy sat back and laboriously unwound rags to reveal a twisted foot with the toes curled under the arch.

Extending his left hand, Matthias said, "Eshtol, God healed this hand and made it strong after it had been crushed and crumpled for many years. Do you want to be healed?"

Hope kindled again on the serious young face. "Oh yes."

"Then in the name of Jesus of Nazareth, stand up and walk!"

Eshtol rose and in the instant between his push to stand up and the moment when his weight rested on both feet, his crippled foot grew normal. Like the time Jesus had fed the multitude, Matthias could not see what happened—only the result. It was as if Jesus himself were there.

Eshtol stared at his toes, all ten touching the floor in perfect order. He wriggled them experimentally and then leaped straight up in the air with a whoop.

"The Lord is visiting his people!" rejoiced Zimri. He burst into song. "Oh give thanks to the Lord! Make known among the nations what he has done!"

Eshtol laughed and cried and said, "Thank you . . . thank you," before he dashed out to show the villagers.

David ran after him, but Zimri turned to Matthias and begged, "Tell me more about the Nazarene."

Matthias and Judas stayed to preach about the Kingdom of God for several days before moving to the next village. Over a period of a fortnight they lodged in eight different villages, preaching and healing the sick. Every town welcomed them, but one—Kerioth, Judas' hometown. Some of the young men there belittled Judas, and to avoid trouble, the elders withdrew their hospitality. Jesus had said if any town refused his peace, the disciples should shake its dust from their feet and move on. This Judas did and Matthias could not tell whether his voice shook with grief or anger. They spent that night in a cave.

In the morning Judas berated himself. "I should have left Kerioth to another disciple. I should have known they wouldn't receive me any more than the people of Nazareth received Jesus."

"You couldn't know. It's not your fault."

Judas squared his shoulders and straightened his robe. "You're right," he said abruptly. "They are stiff-necked and arrogant. I don't know why I was homesick when I first went to Jerusalem . . . but I was. I never really liked the city until I met Lemuel. He taught me the value of city life. I owe him more than I can repay. When we return to Jerusalem, you must meet him, Matthias."

Judas habitually walked fast, as though on some pressing errand. Now he walked even faster. Matthias strode along, glad to stretch his legs. He said, "You told me Lemuel didn't want you to follow Jesus. Has he changed his mind?"

Judas frowned. "He thinks the Master is misleading me." Then he chuckled. "But he'll see I'm right when Jesus declares himself . . . Matthias, did you ever dream healing would come through your hands?"

"That seems more incredible than the miracles themselves."

"To think God grants us power like the power of Jesus!" The intensity of Judas's zeal gave a ring of authority to his voice. "Even demons obey us. And Lemuel thinks I'm being misled!" Iscariot threw back his head and laughed.

"Didn't you tell me Lemuel was a member of the Sanhedrin?"

"Yes. Why?"

"In view of the warrant for Jesus' arrest, wouldn't it be wise not to see him until Jesus declares himself Messiah?"

Iscariot slowed and drew his hood tighter against the cool wind. "Perhaps," he said.

They walked on in silence.

Just when I think I'm getting to know Judas, reflected Matthias, *he becomes as elusive as a coney hiding in the rocks.*

Glancing at his companion's set profile, Matthias realized Judas had not reconciled the conflict between filial devotion to Lemuel and commitment to Jesus.

Well, I know how that feels, Matthias mused. With the return of his sense of well-being had come also the attacks of longing for Miriam.

A fortnight later Matthias and Judas Iscariot rushed through the night toward Emmaus.

Upon their return to Jesus at Bethany, Matthias had learned that Grandmother Hephzibah lay gravely ill. Jesus had said, "Go to her, and as you have done for others these past weeks, heal her in my name."

Iscariot had insisted on accompanying Matthias. Now, hurrying to keep up, he panted, "How old is your grandmother?"

"Past her seventieth year."

They had crossed the Kidron and were skirting the south wall of Jerusalem with at least two hours separating them from their destination. Matthias lengthened his stride.

"You must be very fond of her," Judas puffed.

"Yes. She was sometimes even closer to me than Mother. Not dearer, but . . . she always understood how I felt. She made me work my damaged hand and brought some life back to it. And when Father commanded me to give up ironsmithing and go to the School of Hillel, Grandmother stood against her own son until I could bring myself to submit to his wishes."

The miles seemed endless, but finally the last long hill lay ahead. Matthias ignored his burning leg muscles. Judas doggedly kept up with him. A half-moon lit the mountain road.

At the top of the ascent, Judas said, "Jesus assured you she would recover, didn't he?"

Matthias almost stopped in his tracks. Judas was voicing his own nagging fear that somehow he might be too late. "He said to heal her," Matthias answered. "Of course she will recover."

The road wound around the side of the mountain, snaking into tumbled ravines and out around weathered shoulders and outcroppings of limestone. Emmaus now lay in view, a splash of organized stones defined by moonlight on a distant slope.

By the time they reached the village, the moon had dodged behind a cloud bank, throwing the streets into blackness. Matthias could barely make out the squat form of his mother's and grandmother's little house. In spite of Jesus' assurance that Grandmother would be healed, he had to fight down a growing fear. At the gate he hesitated, dreading what he would find in the house. He said, "Thanks for coming, Judas. You've made this journey more bearable."

"I couldn't let you come alone. After our mission together, I feel like your family is mine."

Matthias squeezed Iscariot's shoulder. "And yours is mine, my friend." One last time he reminded himself that Jesus had said Matthias would be empowered to heal Grandmother. Then he strode across the small garden, knocked gently, and called, "Mother, it's Matthias." Hearing no response, he eased up the latch and entered.

Inside, in dim lamp glow, he saw his mother, Rachel, huddled against the wall on a pallet beside his grandmother's bed. He crossed the room and dropped down beside her.

"Mother," he whispered.

She jumped. "Oh, Matthias, I'm so glad you've come." She threw herself into his arms and began to weep.

"There, there," he soothed. "Jesus sent me. He says she will be all right."

"Oh, he doesn't know how stricken she is . . . she can't speak . . . she can't hear . . ." She shook her head in despair.

Matthias held her close for a moment, and then released her gently and turned to Hephzibah. Her shrunken body scarcely rumpled the robes under which she lay. Matthias groped for her hand, found it, and lifted it to his lips. In the shadows surrounding her eyes he could see her lids half-closed. Her hand lay lifeless in his.

This second mother had seemed indestructible. Old as she was, he'd never faced the thought of living without her.

"Grandmother, it's Matthias. Can you hear me?"

No hint of a response.

"Grandmother, I've come to help you." She gave no sign that she heard. Her unseeing eyes filled him with anguish. She looked as if her spirit already had left. He pressed his forehead against the tiny hand he held and struggled for composure.

Judas came and knelt beside him. "The Lord said to heal her," Iscariot murmured. Matthias, unable to speak, began to shake with silent sobs.

Judas leaned toward him, hesitated, and then reached out and gripped Hephzibah's arm. "Grandmother, in the name of Jesus, arise!" he commanded.

The lifeless fingers in Matthias's grasp tightened. "Matthias?" Wide awake, she looked up at him. "Matthias, what are you doing, waking me in the middle of the night? Rachel, why are you carrying on like that? I was having the strangest dream . . . who is this?" She broke off and pointed at Judas. "You surely don't expect me to arise in the presence of this man."

"Grandmother, Jesus has healed you!" Matthias cried.

"Oh . . . is that Jesus?"

"No. No, this is my friend, Judas. It was in the name of Jesus that he healed you."

Her alert eyes studied their faces in the lamplight. "I dreamed I heard the most beautiful music . . . many voices singing . . . and then a great voice cried, 'Jesus!'" She put her hand to her head. "You woke me too quickly . . . You say I was sick?"

"Very, very sick," Matthias answered.

Rachel stopped babbling thanksgivings and added, "For two days you've not known me, Mother!"

While they explained as best they could, Hephzibah listened, enthralled. At last she straightened on her pillows. "Rachel, we must thank God. Matthias, you lead us. You sometimes pray as well as my son Aaron did." Her eyes twinkled with her old enthusiasm for mischief.

Matthias closed his eyes, lifted his hands over them, and raised his face to the heavens. "Oh Lord God of Israel, may all the Earth praise you. Thank you for delivering our souls from death, our eyes from tears, our feet from stumbling. Thanks be for Jesus in whose name you heal, and thanks be for Judas, a true friend in time of need . . ."

Seventeen

From Emmaus, Matthias and Judas walked to Jerusalem, knowing Jesus would be there on the morrow to attend the Feast of Dedication. Like everyone else driven by the first winter chill, they walked fast and spoke little. Even the Romans did not linger on their rounds. The aggressive slap of their sandals on the paving stones passed by and faded with surprising abruptness.

Before the two disciples reached the main street to the upper city, Matthias urged, "Come with me. My sister will want to meet the man who brought healing to Grandmother . . . I can't thank you enough, Friend, but I will keep trying."

"Please," Iscariot protested. "You would have done well without me. I . . . I fear I'm sometimes too quick to step in." His intense face held a troubled look, which Matthias had learned to recognize as the beginning of a bout of despair. Judas seemed to fall into misery at times when many men would be rejoicing. Now he was staring bleakly ahead.

"You obeyed the Lord," Matthias argued. "I did not. All I could see was how deathly ill she looked."

Iscariot softened. "I know." Then impulsively he offered, "If you will come meet Lemuel, I'll come meet your family."

Above the cheese shop the family bustled them in, settled them in the most comfortable chairs, and plied them with questions. Matthias took care not to show his love for Miriam by any stolen glances or special words.

"Did you get our message?" Hannah asked. "Have you been to see Grandmother? I didn't dare go, with my time so near."

"Grandmother is well," said Matthias. "But if it weren't for Jesus and Judas, we would have lost her."

Miriam lost her aloof look and surveyed Iscariot with sharp curiosity.

"Oh, Matthias!" Hannah cried. "What happened?"

Matthias, using both hands for emphasis, told them how Grandmother had been healed. Miriam followed his every gesture with wide eyes. Her lips were parted, as though her mind seethed with questions. Yet when he finished, she said nothing.

Cleopas exclaimed, "Jesus must be Elijah come back, as Scripture has promised!"

"But when we knew him in Nazareth he was like other boys," said Hannah.

Judas responded, "Jesus may have seemed like other boys, but he is not like other men. He is destined to have the whole world at his feet."

Matthias added, "God has given him great power." Then he told what had happened when the Seventy went out in Jesus' name. "You can't imagine what it was like to see people healed just from speaking in his name. At our command even demons released their victims!"

"He must be the Anointed One!" gasped Cleopas.

Miriam interjected, "Then why doesn't he come out of the wilderness and free us?" She confronted Matthias. "You walk with your head under a bushel. Only last week the Romans arrested Ephraim, the innocent only son of our neighbor, and condemned him to the galleys. Surely the true Messiah would not let our oppression continue while he wandered from one small village to another!"

"Jesus says God has his own time," Matthias explained, hoping to persuade her with the answer the Master had given him.

Her mouth tightened. Grudgingly she admitted, "I can't ignore the fact that he healed your hand, and you say he healed Hephzibah. But what about the rest of us? What about Ephraim in the galleys, and our neighbor's little daughter Judith, ravished by a Roman swine and thrown to . . ." She clamped her teeth over the unspeakable words. "And what about Joel? Did Jesus help him? If he has the power you say and doesn't use it to end our suffering, I say he isn't from God. He's not even a prophet."

"If only you would come listen to him, you would see he was more than a prophet," said Matthias, keeping his voice steady.

"I doubt it," she answered stiffly. She hid herself from him with a veil of coldness.

"You refuse to look honestly at Jesus," he accused.

Hannah looked uncertainly from one of them to the other. She touched Matthias's arm. "Surely you will eat with us."

From the corner of his eye Matthias detected Iscariot shifting his feet like a tethered goat. "Nothing would be more pleasant, but as far as I know, Neriah has not been muzzled. And I promised to go with Judas to meet his friend."

Cleopas said to Iscariot, "Our home is your home. We would be honored to serve you."

Judas smiled. "It is I who am honored, and I regret I can't linger tonight."

For some reason Miriam cast a look of dislike and distrust toward Iscariot. For a horrifying instant, Matthias thought she would negate her brother's words.

While Cleopas and the others followed Judas to the door, Matthias fell in step with her. "I owe much to Judas. So does Hannah," he said lightly. "I had hoped you would like him."

"What does it matter? Your hopes and mine differ greatly."

"I hope you will be my friend again."

"How dare you suggest 'friendship'?" she spat. "As long as you follow Jesus, I see no hope for you. I don't believe in him and I doubt that you would if he hadn't been a boyhood friend."

"Miriam, no mere man could do what he has done."

"Rabbi Ebed says his power is from the prince of demons, and that he is a sorcerer. I find it easy to believe Jesus has cast a spell on you. If he be from God, why do our rulers denounce him? Why do our most learned men refuse to recognize him?"

"I can't speak for them. But as for me, I will stake my life on him."

"Then you are a fool!"

"For him, I would be willing to be a fool!"

She groped for words. "You . . . you're impossible!"

The air between them crackled with their anger.

Matthias excused himself. With a quick farewell he followed Iscariot downstairs.

The stark exterior of the house of Lemuel ben Adar concealed a private world of immense wealth. Judas had not exaggerated when he had said Lemuel could be the wealthiest man in Jerusalem. The massive stone walls could have been built by Herod himself. The interior expressed luxury far beyond anything

Matthias had seen in his years of delivering rugs to mansions. Matthias wondered about the nature of Lemuel's business and his interest in Judas.

Servants in costly robes guided the travelers to a dressing room furnished with ornate basins of water, towels, and a variety of clean tunics and soft woolen robes. A flowery fragrance filled the air.

"Is this the way they always greet you?" Matthias asked.

Judas laughed, his face boyish with excitement. "After my long absence Lemuel will have a feast set out," Iscariot raised an eyebrow, "in honor of my return."

"Like the homecoming of a son?"

"No. Not like Shebuel treated you," said Judas, his voice heavy with an undefinable emotion. "But one day he may . . . when he sees for himself who Jesus is."

They bathed and changed to soft, warm tunics and robes. Supple leather sandals cradled their calloused feet.

A vermilion-robed Nubian slave appeared at the door and escorted them through palatial halls. Matthias noticed countless Oriental rugs and enameled jugs and bowls crafted from gold. Through spacious archways he saw Roman and Greek chairs and tables more appropriate to a foreign palace than a Jewish residence. All this could remain unknown to the rest of the city only because Lemuel possessed the power to avoid street gossip.

The black man paused and bowed them into a room—a very Jewish room. It contained Spartan chairs, stools, chests, heavy iron lampstands, and several low tables with mats and cushions arranged for sitting. On the walls hung woven Hebrew banners.

At the far end of the room a man robed in black and white rose to greet them. Judas rushed forward and knelt at his feet.

"Get up, my boy. It does these old eyes good to see you." Lemuel's voice sounded strong for an old man. He embraced Iscariot and kissed him on both cheeks.

When Matthias approached, the older man seemed to take in everything about him in one piercing glance.

"Sir, may I present my good friend, Matthias ben Shebuel?"

Lemuel smiled and extended a hand. Then taking them each by an arm, he led them to the table from which he had risen. "I'm glad Judas brought you,

Matthias. You are most welcome." He emphasized *welcome*. His warmth seemed genuine.

The older man waved them to the cushions. "Come, dine with me. And you, Judas, tell me what you have been doing these many months since I last saw you."

After the washing of hands, Lemuel asked Judas to offer the blessing. Then while Judas described miracles he had performed through Jesus' power, servants glided in and out with spicy foods and wine. Lemuel listened, nodded, questioned, and remained noncommittal. Rather than being antagonistic toward Jesus, he seemed remarkably tolerant.

Over his silver wine goblet, Matthias studied his host. The white hair and iron-streaked beard misled one. Lemuel's aristocratic face, with its hawk nose and black brows, revealed no sagging skin. His keen eyes missed nothing. He ordered things for Matthias as though reading his unspoken wishes.

While Judas paused to drink, Lemuel addressed Matthias. "You too have done these things for the Nazarene?"

"Yes."

"Before you followed him, what did you do?"

"I was a rug merchant in the employ of Shebuel ben Azariah."

"Carpets! Ah, you must see some of mine, from India and Arabia as well as Persia."

"Yes, sir. I noticed them."

A canny gleam in Lemuel's eyes belied his gentle chuckle. "So the disciple likes beautiful things in spite of his life of relinquishment."

"I once planned to be a goldsmith, sir."

"Oh? Why did you change your mind?"

Briefly Matthias narrated the facts—the turning points—which had brought him to the present. Judas sipped his wine and watched Matthias and Lemuel with a half-smile and occasionally interrupted to add a comment.

At last Lemuel asked, "So you are not an Apostle?"

"No, sir."

"Would you like to be?" he asked casually.

Matthias answered easily, "After much prayer Jesus chose only twelve. I'm happy to serve him as I am."

Lemuel picked up his wine goblet, swirled the contents, and sniffed appreciatively. He sipped and set it down. "Judas was pleased that Jesus chose him. You are a man of talent. Don't you have ambitions?" His voice remained casual, but his eyes probed.

Judas lowered his feet to the floor and started to sit up. At a gesture from Lemuel, he sank back again, his face a study of discomfort.

"Sir, I don't want anything more than to follow him," said Matthias.

Lemuel relaxed, apparently satisfied. To Judas he said, "You hold the purse for the group. Does your Master gather much money from the people?"

"Some. Enough for our needs and to give to the poor."

Lemuel laughed again. "I never thought I would see you doling out money to the poor. How far will you stray from what I taught you?" His jocular tone was forced.

Judas stammered, "I have not forgotten, sir, but in Jesus I've found a new way, one that will bring us the Kingdom of God." He, whose faith so recently had sustained Matthias, now fumbled for more words, but found none.

Lemuel turned to Matthias, "Forgive me if I seem hard. Money is my business, and Judas is like a son to me. I taught him more than my most responsible stewards. Now he discards my wisdom for the dreams of an impoverished visionary."

"Sir, Judas values your wisdom and your esteem."

"But not as much as he values Jesus." Lemuel lowered his eyes to his cup, but not before Matthias glimpsed a chilling bleakness in their depths.

Judas, who could not see Lemuel's face, reclined, tense and pale, across from Matthias. His despondency had returned.

Matthias sat up. His absence might give them a chance to make peace with each other. "I beg your indulgence, sir. Because of your hospitality, I've lingered too long. My own household waits for me. May I be excused?"

"Of course!" Again the warm host, Lemuel walked him to the door of the room. Judas followed in silence.

Belatedly Matthias remembered his soiled robe in the distant room. "Thank you for the clean garments. I almost forgot that I must change back to my own."

"I will not hear of it. Keep those to remind you of one who values a talented man as much as a talent of money." He laughed at his own little joke.

A moment later, as Matthias followed a servant down the long hall, he heard Iscariot exclaim, "My Lord, forgive me! You know I could never forget you and what you've done for me."

Distance muffled Lemuel's answer, but he sounded appeased.

Judas ought to have explained his commitment to Jesus. Yet perhaps he was wise. In time Lemuel would know who Jesus was.

And perhaps I should take a lesson in diplomacy from Iscariot. My own frankness has hardened Miriam against Jesus and against me.

Matthias marched out the gate of the great house and nearly collided with a man coming in. The long tassels of a pharisaical shawl swung incongruously from beneath his coarse cloak. Matthias whipped around for a second look at the hooded figure. Neriah—here?

Eighteen

The rough cloak and concealed face could not disguise the strut of Neriah bar Elul. He disappeared, walking with the confidence of a man who knew he was welcome.

Had Judas ever met Neriah here? Matthias was tempted to turn back to discover the answer and warn Judas, but the gate swung shut. He turned thoughtfully toward the house of Shebuel.

In the morning Matthias awoke from dreams of Galilee and of crowds of people on sun-baked hills listening to the Master. Even later, on his way to the temple, a feeling of displacement dogged him. He didn't really think about seeing Neriah at Lemuel's house until he saw him again in the temple, where the Pharisee led a second attempt to stone Jesus. This time Jesus quieted the mob with reasoning. Even Neriah dropped his missile.

Later, as the Apostles were leaving the city, Matthias asked, "Judas, do you know Neriah?"

"Neriah?" Judas asked blankly.

"The man who led the stoning."

"Of course not. How should I know him?"

"I thought I saw him enter Lemuel's house last night."

"If he did, I never saw him. Listen," Iscariot protested, "Lemuel is not a believer, but he isn't against Jesus either. After you left, he gave me his blessing and said he thought I was wise to follow the Master."

Matthias clapped Judas on the shoulder. "I'm glad he accepts your decision at last."

Matthias put aside further thought of Neriah, for Jesus led them into Perea, east of the Jordan. There he continued to preach, heal, and cast out demons. As his following grew greater and greater, he warned people to count the cost.

In order to be his disciple, he said, they could not love anyone more than him. If he meant to discourage them, he did not. His name was being praised everywhere, except by the Pharisees and scribes.

Matthias hoped legions of believers in Perea would sweep the Lord to the throne of Israel in spite of opposition by the rulers. But when Jesus decided to return to Bethany because his friend Lazarus was ill, Matthias felt it was too soon. Jesus must have agreed, for he journeyed quietly, attracting no attention.

Later Matthias wished the whole of Israel could have witnessed what happened in Bethany. His mind staggered with fresh shock each time he thought of it. Jesus had raised Lazarus to life after the man had been dead in the grave for four days!

On the heels of some of the mourners who had come out from Jerusalem, Matthias rushed to tell his family, hoping Miriam would believe at last. To his disappointment the family had invited Hiram to dinner. Matthias ordered them not to reveal his presence and went downstairs to wait for Cleopas. Cleopas spread out a pallet for him, and Tamara sent him a bowl of hot food and a full wineskin.

From above, voices drifted down, Hiram's carrying most clearly, punctuated by Ethan's laughter, while Matthias tossed irritably on his makeshift bed, wishing he had stayed where he belonged—with Jesus. Then the long day's walk and Tamara's cooking combined to make him sleep.

Cleopas's voice awakened him. An oil lamp brought a warm twilight to the cluttered room. "I thought Hiram would never leave. Father was no help, laughing at all his stories." Cleopas placed the lamp on a chest and sat down beside it.

Matthias stretched and sat up. "I didn't think I'd fall asleep after what happened today," he muttered, running his fingers through his hair. He grimaced and shook his head. "My mouth is as dry as an east wind in the month of Ab."

Cleopas snatched up the still full wineskin and thrust it at him. "What happened?" he demanded.

Matthias let a mouthful of wine awaken his mouth and moisten his throat, took another swallow, and handed the skin back to Cleopas. He shifted to adjust his back to the edge of a chest behind him.

"Well?" Cleopas asked.

"I wish you had been there. I wish you could have seen it with your own eyes."

"Just tell me."

Briefly Matthias described the events leading to Jesus' journey to Bethany.

"The Apostles were right to fear for their lives in Judea," said Cleopas. "There is an undercurrent of evil in this city that bodes no good for Jesus. The next time the rulers move against him, they will make certain of their own success before they start."

Matthias smiled, fully awake now, and filled with the excitement of his news. "Wait until you hear what the Lord did," he countered. "When we reached Bethany, Lazarus had been dead for four days . . ."

"Oh, I'm so sorry . . ."

"No, let me finish. Jesus told Lazarus's sisters, Martha and Mary, that he was the resurrection and the life, and that anyone who believed in him would never die. Then he asked to go to the tomb. On the way he wept and groaned to himself. It sounded like he whispered God's name. Then when we reached the tomb, the breeze seemed to dry his cheeks in an instant. His face took on the look of a king, and he ordered us to roll back the stone.

"Simon and Andrew and I were the closest, but before we could obey, Martha cried, 'Lord, the smell will be offensive.' "

Cleopas grimaced. "You're not going to tell me Jesus defiled himself by entering the tomb!"

"I thought the same thing when he told us to open the grave. I hoped he would not go into that unclean place. He hushed Martha, reminding her of what he had said to her about believing in him, and ordered us to roll back the stone.

"So we put our shoulders to it, and Martha was right. My stomach writhed at the odor that poured out. I felt like it would take more than ritual cleansing to purify me.

"Then Jesus said a brief prayer and called, 'Lazarus, come out!' "

Matthias straightened and leaned toward Cleopas. "The odor of rotten flesh vanished, and Lazarus walked out of that tomb, grave clothes and all." Matthias grabbed Cleopas's arm and shook him. "He lives! A man who was dead for four days is alive tonight in Bethany!"

Stunned, Cleopas sat as mute as the crowd at the tomb had been. Then, just as they had, he exclaimed, "Jesus *is* the Son of God, the Messiah!"

"Yes!"

Cleopas peered at Matthias in the dull light. "What will he do now?" he asked in an awed voice.

Matthias straightened and leaned back again. "I don't know. Surely the people will crown him king soon, even if he doesn't declare himself Messiah."

"But what of the rulers? What of Rome? Can freedom come without bloodshed, even for the Messiah?"

"I don't know, but I will follow where he leads."

"So will I." Cleopas clasped Matthias's hand, man to man. "You must let me know what I can do."

"I will. For the present, keep quiet. When you hear reports about Lazarus, feign ignorance. I can't believe Jesus would do anything that could bring harm to believers, but plan for the safety of your family. Rome and Herod will not want to forsake the path of bloodshed. And keep your eye on Hiram. I caught him spying on me."

"Hiram!" Cleopas pursed his lips and gave Matthias a troubled look.

"What's wrong?"

"You don't know how much he has become a friend of the family. Father dotes on him. In fact, tonight I began to suspect Father may give him Miriam's hand, even if she does not wish it."

"Oh no," Matthias gasped, "not against her wishes and his own promise."

Cleopas sighed. "If you care, you'd better do something. You have not acted like a suitor. Hiram is ever present and charming and could provide well for a wife."

"But not against her wishes," groaned Matthias.

"Why don't you speak for her? I think it's you she wants. She hasn't been herself since you took your leave during the Feast of Tabernacles.

Matthias closed his eyes and shook his head. He repeated the refrain he had recited to himself for so long. "What would Neriah bar Elul do to my wife? Or what would he do to our children?" He opened his eyes and lashed out savagely, "Don't you see I can't protect her? Until Jesus comes to power and we are free of the likes of Neriah, I have no right to speak for her."

Cleopas had no answer. When he left, he gave Matthias an understanding pat on the shoulder.

Nineteen

Matthias lay wide awake in the cheese shop storage room after Cleopas left him, tormented by the thought that Miriam could be betrothed against her wishes. If only Jesus would take his place on the throne . . .

It seemed that all life was revolving like a chariot wheel gathering speed for battle. At the hub stood Jesus, affecting everyone and everything.

The people of Israel are the spokes, thought Matthias. Miriam and I, Judas and Lemuel, Hiram, Neriah—for all of us everything pivots on what Jesus does.

He stretched wearily. Cleopas was right. Unless the Lord made a miracle, neither Herod nor Rome would surrender without a battle. And most Jews lived for the day they could fight for freedom. With a shudder Matthias prayed, "Lord, don't let it be by the sword."

Somehow Matthias finally slept.

In the morning he was up and ready to leave by the time Cleopas came downstairs and invited him to join the family for morning prayer.

Matthias declined. "I must go. I've already prayed alone. Please don't discuss Lazarus with the family. If I'd known about Hiram, I wouldn't have come."

"But surely they will hear. You said people from Jerusalem witnessed the miracle."

"Let them not hear from us, anyway. Until the Messiah is king," said Matthias, "let's guard our tongues."

"Until the Messiah is king," answered Cleopas, and the way he said it, it was like a salute, like the way the Romans proclaimed, "Hail Caesar."

"Cleopas!" called Hannah from above. "Tell Matthias that Judas Iscariot has come for him!"

"What can he be doing here?" exclaimed Matthias.

"Let's go see." Cleopas started for the upper rooms.

"No. Send him down and we'll leave by the alley."

"You don't want to say good-bye to the family?"

"I'm tired of good-byes. Just give them my blessing."

Cleopas nodded. At the upstairs door he raised his hand and repeated, "Until the Messiah is king." This time it was more like a prayer than a salute.

"Matthias! I hoped I'd catch you before you left!" Iscariot called excitedly from the stairs. His voice carried so loudly he could be heard on the street.

"Judas! Quiet!" Matthias hurried to him and pulled him toward the storage room's outer door. "What are you doing in Jerusalem?"

"After you left I came also. It's a good thing I did. You should have seen Lemuel's face when I told him about Lazarus. Matthias, Lemuel is a believer, and he wants to help Jesus! With his help Jesus will have no trouble." In a state of elation, Judas couldn't stop talking. "I never told you of Lemuel's true power, Matthias. He can command numberless people, including people in high places, and receive instant obedience. Lemuel asked me to bring you to see him before we rejoin Jesus."

"Me? Why me?" Matthias asked, trying to make sense of Iscariot's barrage of words. Because Judas showed no inclination to speak quietly, Matthias urged him on out into the alley.

His friend jabbered on, paying no attention to where he was. "He likes you and wants to hear from you what happened at Lazarus's grave. I told him you helped roll the stone away."

"But we must return to Bethany."

"No need to hurry. Jesus is staying with Lazarus and his sisters tonight and perhaps longer. Believe me, it's worth our time to comply with Lemuel's wishes."

Before Matthias could answer, Cleopas strode downstairs into the alley and handed Matthias a Galilean dagger—the brass-handled one Matthias had made and given to Miriam.

Matthias's fingers closed automatically on the hilt as he asked, "Why is she giving me this?"

Cleopas shrugged and shook his head. "She said you needed it more than she did. At first I thought she was angry, but when I looked at her closely she wasn't."

But as far as Matthias was concerned, Miriam had sent an unmistakable message. The return of his gift severed the last thread of any bond between them. She was choosing Hiram. He tucked the blade under his leather girdle and covered it with his robe. "It is well that I came after all," he said slowly.

"Lemuel is waiting," prodded Iscariot.

Matthias stopped arguing. What did he risk? His time would be spent better there than it ever had been in courting Miriam. And for all he knew, God might use this rich man to further the Kingdom. He gestured to Judas. "Let's go."

Judas led the way. Matthias trudged along, the pressure of the dagger against his ribs reminding him with every step that he had lost Miriam. Until now he hadn't realized how much he had hoped she somehow would be waiting for him when Jesus finally declared himself.

At Lemuel's mansion the same Nubian slave guided them to his master. This time the rich man greeted them in a cubicle close to the gate. The room displayed none of the luxury Matthias had seen in the rest of the house. Wooden Roman chairs filled the limited space. On one, which looked like a throne or judge's seat, sat Lemuel.

Though it was near midday, lighted torches held sentinel positions on each side of the group of lesser chairs. At Lemuel's left on a small table lay a stylus, a pen, an ink bowl, a scroll, small sheets of papyrus, and a lighted lamp. A bench completed the usual outfitting for a household scribe.

Without rising, Lemuel beckoned them to the smaller chairs facing him. His lean features softened in a cordial smile. He said, "Again you honor my house with your presence, Matthias."

"It is my honor, sir." Matthias inclined his head in respect and sat where directed.

The Nubian dropped to the scribe's bench and began mixing ink. At Matthias's startled glance, Lemuel explained smoothly, "I hope you don't mind. I have asked Demas to record the facts of this astounding report."

Judas grinned, amused at Matthias's cautiousness.

"I assure you this is only for my own information," Lemuel explained. "I've made it a practice to record important events. I fancy myself a historian of sorts." He chuckled as though at himself. "Surely you will indulge me in this."

"I was just surprised, sir."

Lemuel continued to smile, but his eyes questioned Matthias. "No. I think you do not trust me. If I am to be of any help to your Master, you must learn to trust me." He turned to Judas. "Tell him, my boy, what I've done to show my support for Jesus." Judas dropped his amused look and said, "He has given us a hundred pieces of gold for the purse."

"Gold!" Matthias exclaimed.

Lemuel laughed appreciatively. "I see a glint in the eye of our would-be goldsmith! Even in coin it is beautiful, is it not?"

Caught off guard by this startling information, Matthias searched the keen face above him for a sign of commitment to the Lord.

Lemuel grinned with open delight. "Your Master has captured my imagination. If he can do all Judas claims, he possesses power that must be recognized. May my eyes not greet another dawn if I neglect so great a man! Will you tell me exactly what happened yesterday in Bethany?"

Because Judas already had revealed the miracle, Matthias relented. Adding his own details could scarcely cause harm.

While he recounted the scene at the grave, Lemuel interrupted several times to ask for specific details. How long between Jesus' call and Lazarus's appearance? Again, what did Jesus say when he prayed? Did Matthias really smell decomposing flesh? When did the odor disappear? After each of his responses, Matthias heard the scratch of the scribe's pen, but Lemuel's intense interest distracted him from it.

"What did Lazarus say of his experience?" asked Lemuel finally.

"That when he heard Jesus call his name, he awakened as though from a deep sleep and couldn't believe he was bound in burial clothes and lying in a tomb. He was shocked and confused."

Judas nodded. "I questioned him several times. His answers were jumbled, but the fact is that he truly was dead and lives again."

"Yes," said Matthias. "He was dead. And Jesus raised him."

Lemuel rubbed one hand over the other in a peculiar handwashing motion. He nodded slowly and repeatedly while the scribe finished his work. "The evidence of two witnesses," he said. "And it is written. I am in your debt, Matthias. I shall make it worth your while."

"You owe me nothing, sir," Matthias replied. "The way of our Lord is to give without thought of payment. Besides, you have already given to his cause."

"I would do more. Surely there is something I can do for you. Judas tells me there's a beautiful young woman in your life. I will give you a wedding gift."

"I . . . there will be no wedding, sir. Judas was mistaken."

Lemuel raised his brows with a look of speculation. "If you want her, I will get her for you." He leaned forward, graceful and sure. "I can do that, you know," he said softly.

Matthias felt an irrepressible flutter of hope. No. Even if Lemuel could protect Miriam from Neriah, she had chosen Hiram. Matthias said, "Judas misunderstood."

Lemuel leaned back. "I see. But remember you have only to ask. I can be a blessing to those who know me as friend. Isn't that so, Judas?"

"So you have been to me, my lord," Judas answered with a new assurance. He had used that term of honor with the rich man before, but never with the reverence they all reserved for Jesus. Startled, Matthias peered questioningly at him. Iscariot returned his look with a cheerful smile. The raising of Lazarus apparently had mended any differences between him and Lemuel.

None of us will be left unmarked by the Master, thought Matthias again. He wished he had told Miriam about Lazarus after all. It might have made a difference to her too.

Lemuel rose. "You must let me know of the Master's needs."

Judas leaped to his feet. "We shall indeed, sir."

Matthias stood up slowly, feeling that something important had been left unsaid. He couldn't capture the thought that teased to be recognized. Had it to do with the Master . . . with Judas . . . or with Miriam?

As Lemuel walked them to the door, he rested a paternal hand on Judas's shoulder. To Matthias he remarked with pride, "One thing Judas understands is the worth of money. I have no qualms about entrusting my gifts to a purse he manages. He will get value for every denarius, won't you, my boy?"

"Of course, sir." A look passed between them that excluded Matthias.

Lemuel caught Matthias's eye and exclaimed, "I owe your Master much for sending Judas back to me a greater man than when he left. He has come of age, has he not, in these past months?"

Matthias looked at his friend afresh. Judas had changed. His eye seemed steadier, his stance firmer. "Yes," he agreed. "If I am one to judge," he added with a smile, "for we are the same age."

Lemuel laughed. "You must come again, Matthias. And remember I would do you a kindness."

As the two disciples left the sleeping city, they had to evade the Romans on watch. Once they were safely out of earshot, Judas said with contempt, "I wish the Romans could know their days here have been numbered and how few they have left."

Matthias wished he could feel as confident. All he was sure of was that everything depended on what Jesus did.

Twenty

After raising Lazarus, Jesus left Bethany to avoid the high priest, who had decided Jesus must die before the people declared him king and brought the wrath of Rome against the nation. So Jesus, the Apostles, and Matthias stayed in a city called Ephraim through the winter.

Then with the approach of Passover, even though Jesus had talked more about being killed, they all returned to Bethany. His men alternated between fear and the conviction that Jesus could not mean literal death. The fact that he planned to attend Passover seemed to confirm their conviction. Of one thing they were certain, he had demonstrated his power over nature, demons, and people. Now it only remained for him to demonstrate his power specifically over the high priest, Herod, and Rome.

In Bethany, with only the Mount of Olives separating Matthias from Miriam, Matthias grew restless. Was she now betrothed to Hiram? The evening of the first day of the week, he confided to Judas and Simon, "I'm going into Jerusalem tomorrow even if Jesus does not."

Simon, resting beside him on a bench at the side of Martha's and Mary's garden, said, "You shouldn't go before the Master shows himself."

Matthias reasoned, "I'll disguise myself."

Judas jumped to his feet. "I'll go too. I'll need to prepare if the Master chooses to remain in the city at night."

"He and the Twelve can stay at Shebuel's house," Matthias offered.

"Are you forgetting they want to kill Jesus?" exclaimed Simon. "He can't stay where he may be expected."

"Well," replied Matthias, "in light of the death warrant, he shouldn't even be here, let alone go to the temple for Passover."

"I know that," said Simon irritably.

"But you forget who he is," exclaimed Judas, laughing. "The people won't permit the priest's men to take him. And what could Caiaphas do? Rome won't allow him to execute anyone."

Simon shot back, "Yet you heard the Lord say plainly that unrighteous men would seize him and kill him."

"And that he would rise again," added Iscariot. "Does that sound like a real death?"

"I don't know!" Simon exploded, glaring at Judas.

Matthias interceded, "Judas does make sense. Simon, you saw Jesus raise Lazarus after he was rotting in his grave. How could the high priest harm one who possessed such power?"

"Jesus says he could, that's how." Simon thrust out his chin with the stubborn passion that had led him into trouble as a boy.

"He's speaking in parables," Judas insisted, ignoring Simon's black look.

"Parable or not," said Simon, "you'd better stay out of the city unless the Lord says to go." He pushed himself to his feet and strode angrily away in the fading light.

"What makes our Zealot so fearful tonight?" asked Iscariot.

"Fear? We've all been unsettled by Jesus' talk of death. And after the way the Lord rebuked Peter, even John doesn't dare to question him." Matthias shifted his weight on the hard stone seat and looked up at Judas. "I can't help but wonder. Sometimes I think, What if Jesus is foretelling his death? Then I can't imagine how anyone could kill him. He is the Messiah."

Iscariot, still standing while Matthias sat, folded his arms across his chest. "He cannot die. Therefore he will not," he said with authority.

Matthias leaned back and looked up at him. Lemuel was right. Judas had matured. How else to account for his confidence? Matthias wished again he could feel that sure. But he was not one of the Twelve. Jesus probably had known from the beginning that he wasn't capable of that much faith.

Judas said suddenly, "Matthias, Sabbath has ended. Let's go now."

"To Jerusalem? Tonight?" He searched the shadowed planes of Iscariot's face for signs of jesting.

"Why not? We can return before dawn and miss nothing here."

It took Matthias only an instant to decide. He longed to see Miriam, even if she were betrothed.

❋

An hour later inside the dark city, the two disciples clasped hands like boys on an adventure and parted, Judas to see Lemuel and Matthias to see his family.

Above the cheese shop, in answer to his knock, Cleopas pulled him into a dark and quiet house.

"Here," Cleopas urged, "be seated. Everyone else is asleep . . . what with a new baby . . . but I haven't told you. You are the uncle of a strong, healthy girl. We've named her Priscilla, for my mother."

"Thanks be to God! How is Hannah?"

"More beautiful than ever, and little Priscilla is the image of her mother."

"And how is Miriam?"

Cleopas raised his eyebrows and said noncommittally, "She's tired. She's assumed much of Hannah's work, and the baby wakes all of us at night lately. But let me fetch food and drink. Then we can talk," said Cleopas. He disappeared, but returned quickly with his hands full.

Over the wine and bread Cleopas asked, "When will the Master come into the city?"

"I'm not sure. That's why I came tonight. I had to know how you fared, and, in truth, Miriam has been on my mind. Does she now believe in Jesus?"

"Miriam." Cleopas sat his goblet down and gestured with both hands. "Hannah is a believer. So are Father and Tamara, but Miriam . . . sometimes I think she argues just to be arguing."

"I thought she'd surely see the truth when she heard about Lazarus."

"No. I keep praying she will. She had a winter fever, and since then she seems weary of everything. At first the baby cheered her, but now she holds her only when Hannah asks."

"I wish you had sent me word!"

"I didn't know where you were."

"Of course. I forgot." He had worried about Neriah hurting Miriam, but never had considered that she could fall ill. "But now we can take her to Jesus!" he exclaimed.

Cleopas shook his head. "She'd never go. And the physician has assured us that she is over the illness." Cleopas's brows came together. He fingered his goblet thoughtfully. "Hiram's been here more than ever," he remarked.

"Are they betrothed?"

"Not yet. She's been too ill."

"Does she look on Hiram with favor now?"

"She smiles for him. She . . . oh, how can I know the heart of my sister? She's not like my Hannah, who could not conceal anything if she tried."

"Miriam feigns likes and dislikes? I would expect that more of my sister than of Miriam."

"Perhaps it's not given to brothers to understand their sisters." Cleopas smiled, tore a piece of bread from the loaf, and handed it to Matthias. "Eat, Brother, you look tired."

Matthias took it, but did not eat. "Do you think she will see me?"

"Miriam?" Cleopas asked with his mouth full.

"Of course, Miriam!"

Cleopas sipped the last of his wine and set aside his empty goblet. "In this house she will find it difficult to avoid seeing her brother's brother-in-law," he answered dryly.

Matthias frowned. "You jest and I'm worried about her."

Cleopas sobered. "I will make sure she sees you. Now tell me about Jesus."

Trying to set aside his anxiety over Miriam, Matthias told Cleopas of recent teachings and healings. When at last Matthias mentioned the Lord's teaching about his own death, Cleopas sat in stunned silence. Then just as Peter had done, he exclaimed, "But this can't be!"

"So we all have said, only to anger the Master. He says we speak for Satan."

"Then surely he won't come into the city while Caiaphas openly seeks his life!"

"He will come." Matthias leaned over, scarcely able to control his excitement. "Don't you see? Jesus must meet the high priest's challenge. Most of us believe this is how he will declare himself and show his power."

"And you think Caiaphas can't harm him?"

"We believe Jesus speaks of a symbolic death. He will die to the homeless way of life he's led these past three years and to the rejection he's suffered from the very ones who should have recognized him. At any rate, just as often as he has foretold his death, he's promised he will rise again."

Cleopas nervously slapped his hand against his fist. "Nevertheless, real danger lurks here for Jesus."

A rap on the outer door brought them both to their feet. "It must be Judas," Matthias explained.

Cleopas opened to Iscariot—and to Hiram.

"Shalom, Cleopas," said the guard.

After greeting Cleopas, Judas turned to Matthias with subdued excitement. "Matthias, Hiram is our friend. Imagine . . . a temple guard who believes in the Lord."

"Shalom," said Hiram. He smiled at Matthias with easy grace. "We've met, have we not?"

"Shalom. Yes, we've met." Where and how had Judas met Hiram? While his mind raced with questions, he accepted Hiram's hand, hoping his own face was as unreadable as the countenance of this temple guard.

Judas, apparently sensing Matthias's wariness, explained, "I met Hiram at Lemuel's. His uncle serves Lemuel as steward over his vineyards near Bethlehem."

Hiram nodded. "I was surprised to learn Judas was coming here. I couldn't let a friend walk alone and unarmed so late at night." He turned his dark gaze to Matthias. "Judas says you wish to leave the city tonight. I'll see you safely to the gates and get you out without undue notice."

Matthias shrugged at Hiram's offer. "We can do for ourselves." He didn't want the temple guard to guess their destination if Judas hadn't already revealed it. And he didn't want the man's company.

Iscariot intervened. "I'd be glad to have him escort us, Matthias."

At the same time Cleopas shot Matthias a silencing glance.

"Very well," said Matthias. Perhaps Judas had good reason to trust Hiram. To Cleopas he said, "Tell the family that I look forward to seeing them."

Hiram stooped to go out the door and descended the dark stairway with ease born of familiarity. Matthias clamped his teeth together in irritation.

Once they were safely out of the city and away from the guard, Matthias breathed easier, but Judas eulogized the man. They had just met, yet Iscariot rejoiced in his friendship. "Don't you see?" he argued as they climbed the Mount of Olives. "Jesus needs believers like Lemuel and temple guards. They are in positions to help him."

Although Matthias had once tried to help Jesus in much the same way as Judas was suggesting, now he balked at the idea. "Jesus doesn't need them. He has power from God."

"He told us to make friends for our day of need," Judas countered. In the impenetrable dark before dawn, Iscariot's voice sounded disembodied, almost alien.

Gruffly Matthias corrected him. "The Master meant for us to make friends of heavenly powers."

Judas grunted and lapsed into silence.

For Matthias the encounter with Hiram had cast a pall on his visit to Jerusalem.

Twenty-One

By the time Matthias and Judas reached Bethany, the sun had leaped up and the western sky had turned a fathomless blue. They joined the others in morning prayer, devoured a quick breakfast, and, without rest, started back toward Jerusalem with Jesus.

A short distance from the city Jesus stopped and sent Nathaniel and Philip into Bethphage to fetch a young donkey. When they brought the foal, Jesus mounted it.

An old man who had trudged up beside Matthias exclaimed, "The prophet Zechariah said our king would come not on a war horse, but riding on the foal of an ass!"

As Jesus rode the colt down Mount of Olives, people recognized him and flocked to him until they formed an immense parade. They sang and shouted praises and laid their garments on the road to carpet the way, calling him the Son of David—the Messiah.

Some glowering Pharisees shoved through the rejoicing throng and demanded, "Teacher, rebuke your disciples!"

Jesus shouted, "If they be silent, the stones will cry out."

"Did you hear Jesus?" cried Matthias to Simon the Zealot.

Simon nodded and shook his clasped hands over his head.

Everything they had prayed for, everything they had sacrificed for, would soon be accomplished. Matthias thought, *Now Miriam will see why I had to serve him.*

Jesus halted the foal. Jerusalem stretched before them in golden beauty, crowned by the dazzling white-and-gold temple. Suddenly the Master was grief stricken. "Oh, Jerusalem," he lamented, "if only you knew peace this day. Because you didn't know the time of your visitation, enemies will encompass you and destroy your children," he cried. His voice broke and he wept.

The people rushed ahead, singing and waving palm branches like banners. Jesus nudged the donkey onward. All the way into the city, the swelling multitude praised him as the Promised One.

Surely Caiaphas would not dare to go against so many people, thought Matthias, but why had Jesus wept for the city? Would there be bloodshed?

That day Jesus taught and healed in the temple with no more interference than arguments from the Pharisees.

In the evening, when the Lord returned to Bethany, Matthias went to his own home and sent Tobias to Miriam with a message. On a bit of papyrus he had scribbled, "Forgive me, but I must speak with you this week. Matthias."

When Tobias returned he appeared at Matthias's door and said, "Miriam insisted on returning with me. She awaits you in the reception room."

"Thank you, Tobias. You always serve me well."

The steward inclined his head in his serious manner and disappeared down the hall. Matthias, still in the rough garb of travel, strode across the courtyard. He felt utterly unprepared for Miriam's unexpected appearance.

She was standing in the center of the room. At the sound of his step she turned slowly and threw back her hood, exposing her russet hair to the warm lamp glow. She was thin and pale, and her eyes seemed to have taken over her face. Matthias's throat tightened.

"Miriam!" He tried to keep his voice steady.

Soberly she appraised him.

He felt if he moved too quickly or approached too close, she'd flee. Where was the vibrant, strong-willed young woman he had known?

"Won't you be seated, please?" he said quietly.

She accepted the chair he indicated. But in a gesture that struck him as defensive, she drew her cloak tightly around her shoulders. "You wanted to see me?" she asked, her voice so low he had to strain to hear her.

"Yes. I wanted to talk—to tell you what happened today."

"Father permitted me to come and sends his greeting." She smiled hesitantly. "You are still a son to him, Matthias."

"I love him . . . and I love you, but not as a brother."

She seemed to shrink within her tightly clasped robe. "Please don't. That has all changed for me."

In a stride he was beside her. He dropped to his knees and picked up her hand. Fragile, cool, and unresponsive, it rested in his. "Then why did you come to me?" he demanded. Impulsively he uncurled her fingers and pressed his lips to her palm. She caught her breath and began to tremble.

"Why did you come, Miriam?" he persisted.

She pulled away from him. Color returned to her cheeks. "I came . . . to try once more to persuade you to stay away from Jesus."

"Oh, Miriam," he groaned, and started to rise to his feet.

She caught his face with both her hands. On the edge of hysteria, she cried, "Matthias, don't you see what's happening? They'll seize him and his men. Please go away and hide yourself. They will kill you!"

"Dear and beautiful Miriam, listen to me. Jesus will soon be King! This is what I wanted to tell you. Our long wait is almost over. Multitudes are praising him as their Messiah. No one can stop him. No one can kill him. I'm in no danger at all." He gazed into her anxious face. "Thousands of Israelites believe in him now. Won't you also believe?"

She didn't answer, didn't even seem to hear. She began to stroke his hair, his cheeks, his beard. She murmured, "If you left him . . . for a season . . . you could return to him later. Oh, Matthias, we could be together," she whispered. "If you left him we could marry."

He caught her hands and pressed her folded fingers against his cheek. It would be so easy to take her in his arms and say yes, even though she was still against Jesus. Jesus would understand his love—his need for Miriam.

"Oh, Lord," he breathed, unaware that he spoke aloud to an absent person. Suddenly, instead of the triumphal entry, so joyous and promising, Matthias remembered how Jesus had wept over Jerusalem. Memory of the Lord's anguish wrenched him away from his own desires. He must continue to wait for Jesus to reign and for Miriam to believe in the Messiah!

Matthias dropped Miriam's hands and stood up. The brokenness between them was so real, Matthias expected to see shards of something precious lying at their feet. Her nearness threatened to drive thought from his head and words from his tongue. Backing away, he sat on a chair facing her.

Impulsively he accused, "You would offer yourself to me as enticement to leave Jesus." The moment he said it, he regretted his harshness.

But she only nodded, her eyes alive again and burning with hope. "If you love me . . . and want me, you will do it."

"Like Samson of old?" he cried, leaping to his feet. "You don't know yet what love is, Miriam."

Wilting, she started to speak, and then closed her lips and slowly rose. When she found her voice, it was surprisingly strong. "I'm sorry I came. I should have known that there was only Hiram."

Astonished and hurt, he raged, "Will you flee straight from me to him?"

"Yes!" she flared. Chin in the air, she marched to the door and demanded, "Tell Tobias I await him at the gate. And please spare me any more of your company."

He did her bidding and retired to his room, feeling bruised and beaten. His ears rang and his eyes burned from lack of sleep. He threw himself on his couch and finally weariness won.

In the morning when he awoke, Miriam's visit haunted him. It seemed unreal that she could have changed so much. Surely she could not love him and then forget him for Hiram. In all the years he'd known her, she'd been steadfast in her affection. Cleopas must be right; she was practicing some kind of a deception. Whatever it was, he would wrench it from her. He set out for the temple, hoping to speak privately with Hiram. The man might know more about Miriam than Matthias had wanted to admit.

When Matthias arrived he didn't see Hiram, but the Court of the Gentiles was in an uproar, and Jesus was at the center of it. He had thrown out the money changers again.

Matthias hurried to the Twelve. Simon whispered, "The Master cleanses evil from this holy place."

"It is against Caiaphas he has moved," said Matthias. "This will lead to their confrontation."

But the rest of the day passed much the same as the day before. Jesus went to Solomon's Porch and taught. As he gestured to make a point, Matthias was transfixed by the Lord's hands. Those hands had healed a blind man and tenderly lifted little children yesterday and now today had overthrown the money changers' tables. They were the hands of a king.

Matthias scanned the responsive crowd. Never had anyone so stirred Israelites without a battle cry or the waving of a sword. Only the Pharisees and scribes continued to argue and try to trap Jesus with his own words. And they failed utterly.

Toward the end of the morning, Matthias finally spied Hiram and elbowed toward the guard. Hiram caught sight of him and shook his head, casting a warning glance toward his fellow guards.

Matthias halted, but kept an eye on him. After a bit Hiram wandered in his direction. When he passed Matthias, he whispered, "Lemuel wants to see you and Judas tonight." Keeping eyes to the front, he strolled on.

There had been no way to ask about Miriam. Matthias bit his lip. He hadn't bargained on being given orders and did not intend to obey. Frustrated, he turned back to Jesus and came face to face with Neriah.

The Pharisee shot him a look of hatred, but said nothing.

Matthias nodded at him anyway, unable to resist a disdainful smile for this enemy, who would prove as insignificant in halting Jesus as a flea on a lion.

Neriah's eyes narrowed, but he made no gesture to express his obvious contempt. Matthias bowed slightly, still smiling, and continued toward the Apostles.

Later in the day, when Jesus was leaving the temple, Iscariot caught Matthias by the arm and pulled him aside. "I saw you with Hiram. What did he say?"

Surprised, Matthias said, "I almost forgot. Lemuel asked to see us tonight."

"I must stay with Jesus tonight, but you can explain to Lemuel."

"I'm not going either."

Consternation crossed the face of Iscariot. "But you must. You're free to go."

"I have other plans."

Judas scowled. "Don't do anything you'll regret. Lemuel can do much to help the Master. He could even make a way for you to obtain Miriam for your wife."

Matthias repressed the desire Miriam's name aroused. Iscariot's unexpected remark robbed him of words. He thought he had concealed his inner conflict even from those who knew him best. Before he could frame a response Andrew joined them. Resting a broad hand on Matthias's arm, he said, "Will you come to Bethany?"

Matthias grinned at the bear of a man. "I was just telling Judas I'd meet you here tomorrow. My mother and grandmother are coming to the house of Shebuel. I'd like to see to their comfort tonight."

After supper with Rachel and Hephzibah, Matthias excused himself to go to the house above the cheese shop.

When Miriam answered the door, he caught her hand. "Come out. I want to talk to you."

He pulled her out onto the narrow stoop and shut the door. Without preamble, he said, "You've been lying to me."

Her eyes widened and she groped for the door latch.

"Stay!" he commanded, catching her hand and imprisoning it in his own. "And don't say a word until you're ready to tell me the truth."

Her mouth quivered. More eloquent than words, her eyes begged him to let her go.

"You will tell me," Matthias insisted. Careless of whether they might be interrupted by the family, he grabbed her by the shoulders. She flinched under his grip. He eased his hold, but did not release her.

She stared at him dumbly.

In frustration he shook her. "I will not leave until I find out why you've been deceiving me. Even your brother has noticed your evasiveness. Tell me what has made you hide yourself in lies."

"Matthias, please don't!" she cried in desperation.

"Tell me the truth."

"It's Hiram," she admitted haltingly. "I did it for you. He promised to keep you safe. He said he would do anything for me . . . so I asked. I promised myself to him in marriage . . . if he would keep you safe."

"Miriam," he gasped. "In the name of all that's holy, how could you?" His hands fell from her. "How could you give yourself to a man you don't love? Even if you can't believe in Jesus, can't you believe in me?"

She stared at him with stricken eyes.

"You will break this pact immediately," he ordered.

Before she found her voice, she was shaking her head. "No. No! I begged you . . . and you left me no other choice." She flung the door open, dived inside, and slammed it shut. The key grated in the lock.

It took Matthias less than an instant to decide. He hurtled down the steps without a backward glance.

Twenty-Two

At the gate of Lemuel's mansion, the keeper greeted Matthias as if he were expected. Servants led him to the simply furnished Jewish room where he first had met Lemuel.

The wealthy man's black brows smoothed at the sight of Matthias. "Matthias, how I hoped you would honor my invitation tonight. Come, be seated." He motioned to a chair at his side. From a small table he poured wine into chased silver goblets. "Judas is detained?" he asked.

"He sends his regrets, sir. He couldn't leave the Master."

For the briefest instant Lemuel's hand froze over the half-filled goblet, and then he poured and handed the vessel to Matthias. "I'm sure Judas knows best," he remarked with a smile. His sharp eyes appraised Matthias. "But perhaps you know better."

"Sir, I must be honest. I come with a need."

Lemuel's smile widened. "I'm glad you took me at my word."

"Sir, you said you could help me obtain the wife I desired."

"Who is the woman and why do you need my help?"

Matthias told him about Miriam and what she had done out of fear for Matthias's safety.

With an inscrutable expression, Lemuel savored his wine. When Matthias stopped talking, Lemuel motioned toward a tray of food. "Eat and drink, my boy. If you were my age, you would know the passions of love are fleeting, but the body's needs persist."

Matthias reluctantly accepted bread and fruit.

Lemuel leaned back again. "There are more important pursuits than loving a woman, and you can have a family without that transient emotion. You remind me of my own foolish youth." He eyed Matthias with sardonic amusement. "What do you wish me to do?"

"I thought, sir, that you might persuade Hiram to reject Miriam's offer. They are not formally betrothed."

Lemuel sat up, refilled his own goblet, and drank of it thoughtfully.

"My lord, she doesn't love him!" pleaded Matthias. Suddenly he heard himself with shock. He had never called anyone but Jesus *lord*.

At last the rich man said, "I'll do what I can. You understand, of course, that I may need your help in return for this sizable favor."

Relief swept over Matthias. Then the import of Lemuel's last words struck him. He blinked. "How may I help you, sir?"

"We shall see," Lemuel answered. "From time to time I need a man of your intelligence."

"But I must serve Jesus first, sir," Matthias warned.

"Of course," Lemuel answered. "Just as Judas does. I understand that. Remember that I too am a believer."

"Yes, sir."

"I think you may rest easy about your Miriam. I'm glad you had the good sense to come to me," Lemuel said.

A few minutes later Matthias walked home with a light step, not even remembering that Lemuel had not said why he'd wanted to see Judas and him.

The next day in the temple, priests, scribes, Pharisees, and Sadducees all tried to trap Jesus into speaking against Scripture and against Rome. They failed, but their hatred deepened, and their rage kept Matthias as alert as a cornered ibex. He wished Jesus would use his power against them, but the Lord taught and then quietly retreated to Bethany.

Matthias went with him, leaving Cleopas to take the lamb to be sacrificed for the family. He hoped that by the time he returned, Miriam would be free.

On the way up the Mount of Olives, Jesus looked back at the temple and warned them it would be destroyed. He told of an end time and of his coming to power after much suffering on Earth.

None of this teaching fits his present reign as the Messiah, thought Matthias in puzzlement.

Then Jesus warned, "In two days I will be turned over to the authorities and they will crucify me."

After such a bitter day in the temple, the Master's words took on literal meaning. Matthias knew Jesus possessed power to overcome any opposition, yet . . . he spoke of crucifixion and of a specific day of execution.

The Lord cannot really die! His eyes met Iscariot's and he read the same cry there.

In Bethany that evening a man whom Jesus had healed of leprosy gave a dinner for the Lord and his men. Martha and Mary helped to serve it. In the midst of the meal, Mary shocked everyone by pouring a costly ointment, spikenard, on Jesus' head and feet and drying his feet with her hair.

On Matthias's right Simon the Zealot gasped, "She's poured out more than a year's wages!"

On his left Judas added, "It could have been sold and the money given to the poor!" His voice rose sharply above the others.

"Leave Mary alone," Jesus commanded. "She has done me a kindness." He turned to Judas and said, "You always have the poor to help if you wish, but you will not always have me."

Judas squirmed, and in the dim lamplight Matthias saw a dark flush creep over his cheeks.

Jesus fixed his eyes on Judas. "Mary has done her utmost for me. She has anointed me for my burial." Matthias saw a warning in the Lord's look. Or was it a plea? Whatever it was, Judas was missing it. He stared sullenly at the table.

Matthias had never seen Judas so afflicted by a rebuke. After all, the Lord had corrected each of them at one time or another. Although Judas had been free of his fits of despair for several months, a wooden look came over him now. Matthias touched his arm. Iscariot did not respond.

As conversation resumed all around, Matthias tried to draw Judas into it, but the offended disciple would have none of it. Soon he excused himself and left.

At bedtime, when Matthias couldn't find Judas anywhere, he decided to return to Jerusalem and look for him there.

Upon hearing of his plan, Simon angrily exclaimed, "Stop nursing the pup, Matthias. After the temper of the high priest's men today, Iscariot would have to be bereft of his senses to walk back into the city alone. There's no point in going there to search for him."

Matthias stiffened. "So you don't care what happens to your brother."

"That's not what I meant, and you very well know it."

"Then what did you mean?"

"I saw how Iscariot behaved at supper. If he's returned to the city, he has intentionally violated Jesus' wishes. The Master made it clear. The danger there is real. Or do you still think he speaks in parables and allegories?" he challenged sarcastically.

Matthias lashed back, "No, I don't. But unlike you, I intend to do something about it."

"Then you are a fool."

While the others prepared for bed, Matthias fastened on his cloak and went out. Simon followed. "Matthias, I beg of you, don't go!"

"You forget that I have lived many years in Jerusalem, Simon. I know it as well as I know the face of the Master." As he talked, he snugged his dagger into his girdle.

Simon grunted. "What a vile comparison! The one is full of good and the other full of evil. Matthias, I feel something terrible will happen to you if you go into the city without Jesus."

"I feel something may happen to Judas if I don't go."

"Go, then," snapped the Zealot. "In the morning Iscariot will wander in from the hillside, and you, if you live . . ." He choked on his frustration.

Matthias tugged his dagger from his girdle and pressed the hilt into his friend's unwilling hand. "Here. You need this more than I. Perhaps it will prop up your sagging courage."

As he strode away, he heard an angry exclamation and the clink of the dagger hitting the ground. Matthias walked on, knowing the Zealot would pick it up again and care for it, if only out of respect for its Damascene steel blade.

The house of Lemuel ben Adar loomed black and silent. Matthias hesitated and then pounded with the knocker. The speed with which the keeper came indicated he had not been dozing.

"I would not disturb your master," Matthias explained through the window in the gate. "But I seek my friend, Judas Iscariot. I wonder if he is here."

The man, whom Matthias knew to be armed like a military guard, looked him over before commanding, "Wait."

A few city night sounds reached Matthias's ears, but beyond the gate silence reigned. Then with a scrape of iron against wood, the gate swung ajar. The keeper beckoned. "Come. Your friend is here."

Matthias crossed through the stone portal into a dimly lit courtyard, where the now familiar Nubian, Demas, bowed and led him down a long corridor into the innermost rooms of the mansion. Matthias sensed he must be in the wing of the house that would face an alley. The servant stopped, rapped on a wooden door, and at a command from within, opened it for Matthias.

Judas and Lemuel were sitting at a rustic table in a small room that looked like a steward's workplace. The single oil lamp sputtering on the table revealed little detail.

"Matthias," said Lemuel. "I wanted to see you, but didn't expect you tonight."

Judas said nothing.

"I was worried about Judas," Matthias answered.

Iscariot replied stiffly, "I'm able to take care of myself."

"I knew you were upset. I just wanted to be sure . . ." To Lemuel he said, "Forgive my imposition. Seeing that Judas is with you, I'll go."

Lemuel motioned to him. "No, please stay. I want to talk to you. Be seated."

Matthias obeyed, studying the two with curiosity. There was an air of tension about them, but at least Judas wasn't frozen in a black spell.

"We were discussing your Master," said Lemuel. "Judas tells me Jesus stirred great anger among the rulers today, but refused to show his real power."

"Yes, sir. He made their wisdom look like childish ramblings, but he taught quietly and then left the city."

Lemuel said, "Judas thinks Jesus will declare himself at a moment when they least expect it—when they think they have defeated him. What do you think?"

Judas was staring, as though silently willing Matthias to agree.

"Why, I don't know. Perhaps Judas is right. I've begun to wonder why the Master waits. We all have," Matthias admitted.

Judas exclaimed, "He's waiting for the right circumstance, so no one will be able to oppose his claim to the throne—not even Rome!" His eyes burned with zeal.

Lemuel leaned forward. "We have a plan to help this come about with the least risk of bloodshed." He leaned closer, fixed his eyes on Matthias, and reminded him, "I have earned a favor from you, and now I ask payment."

"Then you've talked to Hiram?" Matthias burst out.

Lemuel nodded, but said, "Later, my boy. Listen. You must get Jesus to come to your house for Passover supper."

"My house," Matthias repeated. To Iscariot he gasped, "You're making arrangements for Jesus without consulting him?"

"Yes!" cried Judas. "When you hear all of the plan, you'll see it's for the best."

Although Matthias had told Simon he would find a way to help Jesus, Iscariot's arrogance brought him up short. "Judas, I thought of trying to persuade people such as Nicodemus and Lemuel to stand against Caiaphas in the Sanhedrin, but I can't make plans for where Jesus goes or doesn't go. He's our Lord—our Master."

Judas leaped to his feet and shouted, "Don't be stupid, Matthias! We'll just be preparing the way for him. We can do some things for Jesus that he can't do for himself!"

A chill fell over Matthias. He spoke carefully. "In the name of our God, Judas, calm down," he coaxed, "and let's think of a better way to help him."

Judas stood over him, shaking with passion, until Lemuel matter-of-factly ordered, "Judas, be seated. You are becoming overwrought."

Judas had no more than sat when a rap on the door made Matthias jump. At Lemuel's command the door opened and two men, one very tall and the other stocky, appeared beside the Nubian. All three stepped inside and the black man closed the door. The two guests stood for a moment like phantoms and then advanced and threw back their hoods.

Facing Lemuel stood Hiram . . . and Neriah.

Matthias staggered to his feet, knocking his knees against the table leg.

Lemuel said, "You've arrived at an opportune moment. I had hoped my friend Matthias might lend himself to our plan, but he seems reluctant. We will have to do without him. Neriah, Judas will go with you to meet the priests and captain of the guard. Hiram, you manage Matthias."

Matthias swung at the guard with his whole weight, but the tall man didn't waver. Stronger than he appeared and more agile, he clouted Matthias in the ribs with a fist that felt like a hammer. Then in a quick twist he clamped Matthias's arms behind his back and strapped his wrists together with a thong.

"Judas, will you betray the Lord?" Matthias cried.

Iscariot gave him a stricken look and answered hoarsely, "Everything will be all right. Trust me."

"No! No!" roared Matthias. Every particle of his being screamed out against this evil. "They are using . . ."

Hiram stuffed a rag in his mouth and tied another tightly over it. Then the guard swathed his eyes tightly. Matthias twisted from his grip, lost his balance, and fell painfully. Wooden furniture splintered under him.

He heard Lemuel snarl, "Get him out of here! Demas, come help Hiram!"

Hands hoisted Matthias by feet and shoulders. He arched his back and kicked out with all his strength and fell again. In a thundering crash his head hit stone.

Twenty-Three

The distant bellow of the temple trumpets told Matthias it was morning. He had been awake for hours. From the distance of the trumpets, he guessed he was in the lower city, rather than the Fortress of Antonia.

Squatting on the chilly stone floor of a tightly built cell, Matthias tried to think around the throbbing ache in his head. He'd found no possibility for escape, yet he must get to Jesus . . . or get word to him. Of what? He groaned. He didn't even know what the rulers planned.

The truth of what Iscariot was doing had not hit Matthias until he'd seen Neriah. Matthias gritted his teeth. *What a fool I've been, worrying about Judas, while the little viper was slithering to the enemy. If only I'd kept my dagger . . . Oh, Simon, you were right.*

He stood up and stretched to ward off stiffness and weakness. He must be quick if he were to overpower anyone. Even as he thought about it, a scraping sound came from outside his cell.

The door inched open, letting in a sliver of gray light. The tip of a Roman short sword slipped into sight, but the voice was Judean. "Stay back or you'll get no food or water." A swift hand dropped a full skin and a loaf of bread and slammed the door shut again.

Matthias felt across the dirty stones until his fingers bumped the plump container. He fumbled for the flat loaf, tucked it in a fold of his tunic, and took a mouthful of the water. It was potable. He drank more and then propped the skin near the door. He couldn't stomach the bread, but hunger might conquer his squeamishness before he was served again.

Like a caged beast, he paced, stretched, and listened for familiar sounds. Finally he sat down again.

Master, where are you now? Oh, God, keep Jesus safe and get me out of here.

He dozed and prayed and dozed. Someone brought him food again. More hours passed. The whole left side of his rib cage was complaining, his head ached, and his wrists burned where the thong had cut.

He gagged down some bread and again explored every inch of the room, even the corner with the filthy drain. Nothing but solid stone. Sitting down again, he prayed.

A scratching sound made him jump. He had dozed again. A faint scraping at the door brought him to his feet.

Slowly the door opened. "Matthias," came a whisper. "Don't make a sound. I'm taking you out." The unmistakable shape of Hiram filled the door space. Matthias clenched his fists, shifted his weight to the balls of his feet, and squinted into the light.

Hiram tossed him a rough robe. "Keep quiet and put this on."

Matthias held his ground. His enemy could not have become a friend.

"Stop wasting time!" Hiram exploded. "I have to conceal you!"

Matthias grimly obeyed. Even if Hiram meant ill, it would be advantageous to get out of this hole.

Hiram tied a rag tightly over his eyes. "Leave that on."

Matthias felt for the guard's arm and muttered, "Guide me."

For the many turns they made, Hiram might be leading him in circles. At last the shouts and clatter of traffic signaled a nearby busy street. Hiram stopped and removed the bandage from his eyes. They were in an alley near the Damascus Gate.

"Get out of the city," Hiram ordered bleakly. He swung around and retreated down the alley without his usual swagger. Hiram's gloominess surprised Matthias. Miriam was his now. He should be rejoicing. What had happened to make him so stony faced?

Matthias stared for a moment, and then loped to the street and turned back into the city. The shadows showed the day had just begun.

Oh, God, let Jesus be safe in the temple as usual.

Matthias raced on, ignoring the threats and protests from the men he pushed aside. At the street that would lead him most quickly to the temple, he paused to catch his breath and to determine how to proceed through an approaching funeral procession.

Oh, God. It's not a burial. It's a crucifixion.

Roman soldiers prodded a pathetic creature stumbling under his own cross. What had the man done that the Romans would risk riling the Jews with an execution during the Holy Feast Week?

Matthias suppressed the stab of sympathy that could slow his feet and began to force his way past the jackals who enjoyed such sights. Then he realized that no one was reviling the condemned man. They were crying out against the soldiers and wailing as if it were a funeral. As Matthias came near the procession, he had to stop. Marching well-shod feet approached, and then the wavering bare feet of the prisoner, staggering under his burden.

Matthias's stomach twisted in a knot. No crime deserved such a death. A soldier shoved him back out of the way. When Matthias regained his footing, the condemned man had come abreast of him. Under the pressure of the heavy wooden cross, the victim's lacerated back dripped blood. He had survived scourging, yet the Gentile dogs still would crucify him. Anger steadied Matthias's queasy belly. He looked past the tangled mat of hair into the face of the tortured man.

"Jesus!" The cry, half-formed, was torn from his unwilling throat. The Master gazed back at him, his bloodied countenance almost unrecognizable.

"Jesus!" Matthias screamed. Beside himself, he leaped past the Romans and tried to lift the cross. Iron hands grabbed him. His fingers, wet with the Master's blood, slipped. A crashing blow to the back of his head put him down.

The distant clamor of children playing . . . a woman scolding . . . then the pain in Matthias's head swept him to full consciousness. He opened his eyes to an unfamiliar room. He was lying on a pallet. He moved, flinched at the stab of pain, and groaned involuntarily.

"Matthias, lie still."

A soft hand touched his forehead.

"Miriam?"

"Yes. You must lie still and rest."

He turned his head to look at her. The room swirled. Blackness swallowed everything.

He awoke. He had dreamed of Miriam and half-expected to see her. In confusion he peered at his surroundings . . . a humble room he'd never seen before . . . a few chests . . . a mat and cushion beside the pallet on which he lay. Light fell across the floor from two small windows. He started to get up, but dropped back from the sharp pain in his head. When he put his hand to it, his fingers encountered a bandage instead of hair.

Very carefully, he sat up. Then he remembered. They were crucifying the Master.

How long had he been unconscious? He gauged the slant of the sun from the windows. Surely it wasn't yet the third hour. At least he could go and wait with Jesus for the mercy of death.

He lurched to his feet. The room tilted crazily. He must get out before he vomited on the floor. He staggered through the door and found himself in a modest courtyard. Leaning against the wall, he fought a cold sweat that turned his knees to water. Slowly the world righted itself, his heart slowed, and his stomach relaxed.

Then Miriam came. "Matthias!" She rushed to his side, draped his arm around her shoulders, and put a supportive arm around his waist. "You must lie down. You've suffered a bad blow," she said, tugging him back into the room.

He tried to resist and was astonished to feel her strength greater than his. "Let me go to Jesus. They are crucifying him." His voice sounded like an old man's.

She stared up at him, grief-stricken. "It's all over, Matthias. Cleopas just came home and said it was all over."

"But it's still morning!"

"No, evening approaches. He died about the ninth hour, and they've already taken down his body for burial." Her mouth trembled and tears spilled down her cheeks. "Oh, Matthias, I'm so sorry." She drew him into her arms and sobbed against his shoulder.

He stood dry-eyed, unable to express his grief.

Miriam quieted, led him to his bed, and sat beside him, holding his hand until Cleopas came and took her place. He didn't try to talk.

Matthias gave in to despair. *How could Jesus have died? What have I to live for without him? I failed him. I saw Judas change and let my own desires blind me.*

Judas. He would tell the others what Iscariot had done. His fingers hungered to lay hold of the betrayer, but as quickly as his rage had swelled, it subsided, leaving him weak and nauseated again.

Remorse came in a crushing wave, drowning out all else. He moaned, "Why couldn't I have died with Jesus if I could not save him?"

"None of us could have saved him," said Cleopas. "And he wouldn't have wanted you to die with him."

They lapsed into silence.

Miriam returned. "Matthias, you must eat. I brought some broth." She spooned the soup into his mouth while he lay with his head on a cushion. Disgusted that he should, he felt better with the hot liquid in his stomach.

When she had left, he asked Cleopas, "Where are we?"

"Behind the house of Aram, my neighbor."

"How did I get here?"

"A friend who saw you struck down was able to persuade the Romans to release you."

"A friend?" Who had power enough to sway the Romans? "Hiram?" he asked uncertainly.

Cleopas answered, "Yes. Hiram."

Matthias closed his eyes. "I think I'd like to sleep now," he muttered. He hoped everyone would go away and leave him to his private hell, but Cleopas didn't move.

In the morning Matthias felt strength returning. He bathed and dressed in the clean tunic and robe Miriam had left for him.

While he and Cleopas broke fast in the dismal storeroom, Cleopas glanced at Matthias tentatively. "I . . . couldn't talk about it yesterday . . . but I'd like to tell you. I've never seen a man die like Jesus. He refused wine mixed with myrrh to dull the pain. And he asked God to forgive his tormenters. Then when he died, he cried out, 'It is finished!' and just stopped breathing."

Cleopas paused, and then in a hushed voice said, "Matthias, the sky turned black as night, and the earth began to quake. Even the Romans fell to their knees. I heard the centurion cry out that Jesus truly was the Son of God!"

Matthias dropped his head to his hands. *Oh, God, how could you let them crucify him?*

Cleopas continued, as if he had to hear himself say it. "They went to break his legs so he could be buried before the Sabbath, but seeing he already had died, they only pierced his side with a spear and took him down."

Matthias, with his face in his hands, sat hunched with the horror. "I betrayed him," he groaned. "I helped to kill him."

"How can you say that?" gasped Cleopas.

"Because Iscariot betrayed him to the priests, and I went right along, never suspecting him until it was too late. I was with that traitor, Cleopas. I saw him leave Lemuel's house with Neriah to turn Jesus over to the priests."

Cleopas cried, "But you had no part in his crime!"

"I believed Judas. And up to the last moment I agreed with him. What worse betrayal could I commit?"

Twenty-Four

Throughout the day either Cleopas or Miriam sat with Matthias. That night, however, he persuaded Cleopas to go to his own bed.

Before dawn Matthias awoke from a hideous dream in which he was sealed in a tomb. Immediately he remembered. *Jesus is the one in the grave. Oh, God! Why? Why not Judas? Why not me?*

He folded his arms and gripped himself in agony. He had betrayed his dearest friend, the one person who'd always loved him. At last Matthias wept.

When he could weep no more, his thoughts turned to the Apostles. Now that Sabbath had ended, would they be arrested? Would Neriah come looking for Matthias and destroy his family the way he had destroyed Shebuel? And what would Hiram do if it came to saving his own skin? He already had jeopardized his position by releasing Matthias.

Matthias sat up and then cautiously stood up. Neither the pain nor the vertigo returned.

Reassured, he washed, dressed, and stepped outside. Only one desire lived in the deadness of his soul. He must get away from family and friends who might be hurt by his presence.

Before he could proceed, Cleopas appeared, bearing food and wine. Matthias leaned against the doorpost and sipped the wine gratefully.

Cleopas studied him. "You look steady. How do you feel?"

"I've recovered." The fresh, sweet wine gave him quick strength. "I'll go to Emmaus, rest a little, and then move on."

"You can't walk that far so soon after your injury."

Matthias scowled. "Cleopas, do not hinder me. For the safety of the whole family, I must get away from here."

"Then I'm coming with you." Cleopas fastened his huge hand around Matthias's wrist, successfully holding him prisoner.

Matthias glared, but gave in. Together they crossed the alley to the cheese shop storage room and quickly collected a water bottle, light traveling robes, and some cheese. As they started toward the inner stairs to the house, a man's voice—not Ethan's—reached their ears from above.

Matthias groaned. They had moved too slowly. He should have left when he first awoke. He darted back across the storage room to the alley door.

"Wait!" Cleopas hissed. "Listen."

Ethan boomed out, "We must tell Matthias. Run to him, Miriam."

Miriam came scurrying down the stairs. At the sight of them she exclaimed, "Oh!" and stopped abruptly. Her presence breathed life into the shabby place. "You're up! Your friend Simon is here. He says Jesus' body is gone from the tomb and several of the women say angels appeared and told them he was risen, as he had promised!"

Her words seemed to run together and become nonsense to Matthias. His heart sank at the thought that someone had desecrated the tomb and taken away the body. "What?" he stammered.

Cleopas clutched Matthias's arm. "Let's find out the meaning of this."

Matthias followed dumbly. Surely no Jew could have been bribed enough to handle the decomposing body of an executed man. Had the rulers so feared Jesus that they'd paid Gentiles to steal and hide his remains?

Upstairs everyone was talking at once—even Grandmother Hephzibah and Mother Rachel, who had stayed since the Passover supper.

Simon, at the sight of Matthias, strode to his side. "When Judas betrayed the Master and I never saw you, I feared . . ." His voice cracked and he grabbed Matthias in a rough hug.

"Simon!" exclaimed Matthias, returning his embrace. "You know then about Judas. If only I'd listened to you . . ."

Simon released him and shook his head emphatically. "Don't speak of it. I was wrong too. And what could either of us have done? Peter and I drew our weapons, but Jesus stopped us and healed the man Peter had wounded— healed one of those who then took him to his death . . ." Simon's eyes filled with tears.

He opened his robe and pulled Matthias's dagger from his girdle. "I saved this for you, but I have no more stomach myself for ever using a blade again," he concluded hoarsely.

Matthias's fingers closed around the familiar hilt. "What now, Brother? Miriam says his body has been taken."

Simon, as usual when excited, began to gesture with both hands. "Mary Magdalene, Joanna, and the other Mary went early and found the stone rolled back from the door and the body gone. They say two angels told them Jesus was risen, but Peter thinks they are overwrought by their grief."

Matthias nodded in understanding. "Did you go to the tomb?"

"Not yet. Peter and John ran to examine it, but I . . ." He lifted his hands in a helpless gesture. "I couldn't go without knowing if you were safe." He eyed the bandage swathing Matthias's head. "Can you go with me now?"

"Of course."

The whole family argued against Matthias going. Miriam even offered to go in his stead. "It would be safer for Simon," she reasoned. "Who would expect to see one of the Twelve with a woman?"

In the end Matthias won out, leaving Cleopas to watch over the family.

There were few people in the streets, but Simon and Matthias kept their heads covered and their faces averted. From the city gate they could see the Hill of the Skull—a sling's throw from the city's wall—where the Romans liked to display their executions. Matthias shuddered to imagine Jesus hanging there.

Oh, Lord, forgive me. If only I could know you forgave me.

No heavenly answer came. Instead the bright sun, blue sky, and singing birds seemed to mock him with their unsullied beauty. He stubbed his toe and would have fallen if Simon's quick hand hadn't caught him.

At the base of the Hill of the Skull lay a bowl-shaped garden with olive trees and vines growing above a sprinkling of spring grass. Strange that the Master, who had owned nothing, had been laid there in a rich man's grave. As they started down the path into the garden, a slight figure, flying along like a bird, came up the path toward them.

Simon burst out, "Mary! You came back?"

Mary Magdalene paused. She seemed to look through them, past them, as though transported by some kind of rapture. Perhaps her grief had deranged her.

"I saw him!" she babbled. "I saw him as alive as you. I could have touched him, but he asked me not to." She raised both hands above her head in a gesture of worshipful praise. "I've seen the Lord!"

Matthias searched her face for a sign of calm reasoning and found none. "Where, Mary?" Simon exclaimed.

"Down there, by the tomb. I was weeping so hard . . . I didn't recognize him." Her voice trembled between tears and laughter. "He is risen!" Like an ecstatic child, she skipped a little dancing step. "He said to tell everyone." She scurried past them and on up to the road.

Matthias ran down to the open grave, stooped, and entered. Simon followed. Grave clothes lay inside, still suggesting the shape and size of the body they had encased. A wave of grief swept over Matthias. *Oh, Lord! You here? Your body as fragile as mine? You, who walked on water, imprisoned inside the earth?*

Matthias squeezed past Simon and through his tears studied the ground and the grass outside the entrance for evidence. He tried to calculate how many men and levers it had taken to roll the stone back.

Simon climbed out. "What do you make of it?"

Matthias closed his eyes against the sight of the empty grave and shook his head. "I think someone in a position of power has removed the body. As for Mary, you know how excitable she is, and she loved him so much . . ."

On the way back into the city, Matthias plodded at Simon's heels. His ears rang like the shrieking of demons and his head throbbed with pain again. They went directly to the Apostles, puzzled together about what had happened, and finally Matthias returned to his family.

He told them what he'd seen and concluded, "Peter is certain someone has stolen the body. None of the Apostles see any reason to believe the women. Poor Mary Magdalene is beside herself, both laughing and crying." Matthias did not tell them that James had come upon Iscariot's bloated body dangling where he had hanged himself outside the city. They would have to hear that from someone else.

"You agree with Peter, then, that someone has taken Jesus' body to hide it in an anonymous grave?" Miriam asked tensely.

"I'm afraid so," admitted Matthias.

Taut as a strung bow, she challenged, "But why don't you believe the women?"

"If he has risen, where is he?" asked Matthias.

Miriam waited for him to say more. They all waited, as if he should deliver them from their unanswered questions. When he spoke his voice slipped from his control and came out angry. "I only know he's gone, Miriam. I don't know what it means."

She flinched at his outburst, yet she and the others still stood there, waiting for him to say more.

Fighting hopelessness, which could immobilize him, he looked from one to the other of his family. "Please forgive me. I didn't mean to shout. It's just that it's so hard to accept that Jesus is dead . . . like any other man . . . like the thieves who hung beside him. But I can see nothing else."

A bone-deep weariness crept up his spine. He said to Cleopas, "I'd appreciate your company to Emmaus. Sooner or later Hiram will come, and I don't want to be here when he does."

Outside the city, in a beggar's disguise, Matthias's knees threatened to give way with each step. He hunched over his walking stick without needing to pretend. He dragged himself along the road until the mountains closed around him and Cleopas. With the holy city out of sight, they slumped to rest, and then walked on. The midday sun made Matthias's head throb. He sipped water and rested frequently. Cleopas watched him anxiously. "I should have forced you to stay hidden in Aram's storeroom."

"I can walk . . . just need to go slower." He steadied his voice and asked, "Cleopas, when you return, will you search for the Lord's body? I hate to leave Jerusalem not knowing . . ." He thought of Judas's untended body. "I wouldn't want it to be . . ."

"I'll do what I can. If the Sanhedrin or the priests are behind the grave robbery, Reuben may find out and help me."

They walked on silently until Cleopas burst out, "What if the women are right and Mary did speak with him?"

Matthias's heart lurched. "If he rose from the dead . . . he would prove he is more than I ever understood about the Messiah."

"You told me he said he would be killed and rise on the third day."

"But if he rose, where is he?" cried Matthias.

"Hail!" a man's voice called. They both jumped and whirled around. A tall stranger strode toward them, his face shaded by his burnoose. "You were in such earnest conversation that you didn't hear my first call."

Something about the stranger's manner put them at ease. He paced himself to their slow progress. "You seem troubled," he remarked.

"You come from Jerusalem and haven't heard how they killed Jesus of Nazareth, a good and innocent man?" Cleopas exclaimed.

"Ah, that." The man nodded in understanding.

"We hoped he was the Messiah, for he taught as no other man, and he performed mighty works," Matthias explained.

"How slow you are to believe the prophets. Did not the Messiah have to suffer these things?" the man asked evenly. He began to explain Scripture, making it so plain that they wondered why they hadn't seen it for themselves. The man strolled beside them, not looking at them, his face shielded from the hot sun. His voice, low and clear, sounded as refreshing as a Galilean brook.

Matthias thought he must be a great rabbi.

The village of Emmaus came into view at a bend in the road. "Please, sir," begged Matthias, "come stay with us, for the day is nearly spent."

The man nodded agreeably and followed them into town and down the path to Rachel's and Hephzibah's house. Matthias led them over the well-swept path of the courtyard garden and into the house. He quickly fetched water for his guests and pulled aside the window coverings. By the time he'd washed and seated himself, Cleopas had taken out the bread, cheese, dates, and wine he'd carried.

A bee darted into the quiet room on a sunbeam and hovered over the dates. Hearing its buzz, Matthias realized the ringing in his ears had stopped. His headache also had ceased. Gratefully he lifted a loaf of bread from its napkin, handed it to the man, and asked, "Would you honor us with the blessing, sir?"

The stranger took the bread, blessed it, broke it, and with a familiar graciousness, offered them each a portion. On his hands jagged scars extended from wrist to palm. Trembling at the sight, Matthias raised his eyes. The hood no longer concealed a smiling, beloved face.

"Jesus! My Lord!" choked Matthias. He groped for the outstretched hands, but grasped empty air. The Lord was gone. The only evidence of his presence was the broken bread he'd given them.

Twenty-Five

As Matthias and Cleopas hurried back to Jerusalem to tell the Apostles, Cleopas exclaimed, "Didn't you sense when Jesus walked with us on the way to Emmaus that he wasn't an ordinary man? Yet we were blind to him!"

"It was as if he wanted us to understand and believe Scriptures before we saw him for who he was," concluded Matthias. His feet felt as light as his heart. All the way back to the city, every sinew of his body sang a refrain. *Jesus lives and he came to me! Although I failed him, he loves me still!*

In the following weeks Jesus appeared again and again. Matthias went with the Apostles to Galilee, and then back to Jerusalem, meeting with the Lord in each place. At last, from the Mount of Olives, Jesus ascended into the sky and disappeared in a cloud. To see him do so wasn't as startling as the first time they'd seen him appear in a room without using the door, except that this time two men dressed in white appeared to tell them the Lord would return from heaven in the same manner as he had left.

While the rest of the rejoicing disciples returned to their accustomed meeting place in the upper room of a believer's large house, Matthias went to the cheese shop. His presence no longer endangered his family because the rulers were ignoring the Apostles, and, according to Reuben, Neriah had fallen victim to a completely debilitating malady.

Entering from the alley, Matthias surprised Miriam, who was marking and turning cheeses on the shelves. "Matthias!" She dropped her work and hurried to him. "I'm so glad to see you. Have you been with the Lord all this time?"

"You believe!" he exclaimed. Her voice told him so, the way she said "the Lord."

"Yes," she answered. "I know now that Jesus is the Messiah."

"But how did you decide?"

She clasped her hands together, hugging them to her in a girlish gesture of delight. "I couldn't stop thinking about the women who first went to the tomb. Then when you told us about Mary Magdalene, I had to see her. After you and Cleopas left, Simon was good enough to bring her to me."

She gazed up at him as openly as the loving child who had run to him with outstretched arms years ago. "Oh, Matthias, I knew right away that she really had seen Jesus and that he was our Messiah. I felt so sorry for all the things I'd said against him, and for how I'd treated you. Can you forgive me?"

He embraced her gently. "If there was anything to forgive, I forgave you long ago. Will you forgive me for hurting you so often?"

"Yes, yes," she whispered, clinging to him.

In the deepest sense, he thought, we are one. The harmony between them was complete and utterly satisfying. But she still belonged to Hiram. The resurrection had not changed that. He gently released her and retreated a step.

Miriam stepped back. Her green eyes brimmed with questions. He was prepared for anything, except the one thing she asked.

"Have you seen Hiram?"

"Hiram!" Matthias leaned back against the cool roughness of the wall, affecting carelessness. "No. Why?"

"He's so changed. I'm worried about him."

"How has he changed?" Matthias asked brusquely, not really wanting to know.

She frowned and shook her head in puzzlement. "He just seems so distressed. I wish I knew how to help him."

"Help him!" Matthias straightened and tucked his thumbs in his girdle. "Don't you know . . ." Her anxious expression stopped his bitter words. Miriam was the one who had changed. She had come to care for the man she'd once disliked. Instead of telling her how Hiram had helped to turn Jesus over to his enemies, Matthias said, "I wouldn't worry. Hiram is strong."

He caught her hand and pulled her with him into the back of the cheese shop. He called, "Greetings, Father Ethan!" And to Cleopas, "Hail, Brother! I have news." He led Miriam on up the stairs.

Cleopas dropped his work to follow, and Ethan hoisted his bulk swiftly, closed the shop door, and came also.

Matthias told them of the wonder of seeing Jesus ascend to heaven. And while he tried to answer their rush of questions, from the shop below, a ram's horn of a voice bellowed, "Hail! Shalom! The door was unlocked so I came in."

Miriam jumped, more startled than anyone else. "It's Hiram," she said unnecessarily, and walked beside her brother to meet her guest.

While she greeted Hiram, Matthias studied him. To his surprise he saw little evidence of the hardened man who had dragged him to prison the night of Jesus' arrest. When the uniformed guard spied Matthias, however, he began to look more like himself. His mouth tightened to a thin line in his black beard.

"So you've returned," he said.

Cleopas drew Hiram into the room. "Matthias has brought amazing news."

Matthias shot him a warning look, but his brother-in-law continued. "He saw Jesus ascend to heaven."

Miriam, behind Hiram's shoulder, raised her hand to her lips as if she too wished her brother would not reveal so much. With narrowed eyes, Hiram strolled toward Matthias. "You cover lie with lie like a true Galilean," he said. His mouth twisted into a cynical smile, but his gaze wavered and his left lid began to flicker with a rhythmic twitch.

Matthias crossed the space between them in two quick steps. "I don't know what you've heard, but Jesus rose from the grave and has appeared to many people, to as many as five hundred at one time. Now he has ascended to heaven."

Hiram guffawed. The twitch at the corner of his eye kept him blinking. "A convenient solution for a missing body, but not very clever."

Miriam hurried to his side. "Please, Hiram. You know I believe in Jesus. I told you why," she said.

Matthias wanted to drag her away from the insolent guard, but her look held him at bay. To Cleopas he said, "I'll be going to join Simon and the others."

"I'm coming too," said Cleopas.

"Then I'll walk with you both until our ways part," Hiram offered, his voice suddenly congenial.

Cleopas agreed, and Matthias, for the sake of Miriam and his brother-in-law, said nothing.

Out of doors their way led them through the street of metalworkers. In spite of Hiram's company, Matthias's spirits lifted at the sound of an ironsmith hammering hot metal. With each clang his bones remembered the satisfying jolt of hammer against iron.

He glanced at the men beside him. Cleopas still wore the expression of wonder that had fallen over him when he'd heard about Jesus' ascension to heaven. Hiram, however, squinted and blinked with each blow of the ironsmith's hammer.

At the next intersection, beyond the din, Hiram caught Matthias by the arm. "Here we part. But before we do, I want you to tell me man to man—no women's tales—if you really have seen the Nazarene alive again after his burial."

"Surely Cleopas has told you."

"Ah, but he did not know Jesus as well as you did. And he admitted he didn't recognize him at all during the walk to Emmaus." He glanced at Cleopas. "Forgive me, Friend. I don't doubt you believe you saw him." With Cleopas his voice lost its brittleness.

Matthias's inclination was to break free and walk away.

Cleopas, as though reading his mind, grinned and clapped him on the shoulder. "Go ahead and tell him all you've told me."

Matthias quickly described each time Jesus had appeared, concluding, "If I'd seen him only once, it would have been enough. Not only did I know his face and his voice, but I saw the print of the nails in his hands and feet, and the scar from the spear in his side . . ."

"The spear." Hiram gulped convulsively. His face grayed. "Any fool could see he was already dead." He gestured wildly and raved, "Yet they ran him through anyway."

He raised trembling hands and shook them in front of Matthias in an imploring gesture. "They watched it all, just as I did." He shuddered. "Flogging would have been enough, but they crucified him and though he was dead, they stabbed him . . ."

Matthias, incredulous, said nothing.

Hiram raved on. "By the time I came to release you, I despised what I'd done. I haven't been able to sleep . . . the nightmares . . ." He squeezed his eyes shut and pressed his hands to his temples.

It couldn't be, yet Hiram's face mirrored the image of Matthias's own hell of guilt before Jesus had appeared to him at Emmaus. Because Jesus had forgiven him, Matthias gripped Hiram's hand and said, "It's over and he has risen. He forgave me and he will forgive you."

Hiram blinked and peered at Matthias. "You didn't do anything. But for me there's no escape . . . no more than there was for Judas." He backed away. "If Jesus of Nazareth is the Messiah . . . I can only try to atone for my sin . . ." He lurched away.

"No! Wait!" cried Cleopas. He ran after Hiram. The guard shoved him away with a force that sent him sprawling. By the time Matthias reached Cleopas, Hiram had disappeared.

"I must find him," said Cleopas. "He's bent on violence."

"Maybe he means to take his own life, like Judas did."

"That's not Hiram's way. He mumbled something about being duped by someone."

"But surely he must report for duty at the temple soon. He's in uniform."

Cleopas nodded slowly. "Perhaps. I've got to make sure."

They parted and Matthias didn't think of Lemuel until he'd started up the long hill to the house where the Apostles lodged. If Hiram now believed Jesus was the Messiah, he might feel Lemuel had tricked him. Matthias slowed his steps. Could Hiram think that Lemuel's death would atone for his own part in the betrayal of the Messiah?

Matthias stopped. A temple guard in uniform could walk right up to anyone with sword in hand and not be suspect until it was too late. *If he does it, he will pay with his own life,* thought Matthias. *And Miriam will be free of him.* The second thought came unbidden and was irresistible.

Hiram isn't fool enough to try to kill Lemuel, even if he wants to.

Matthias climbed faster. At the door of the house, he reached for the knocker, but stopped short. As upset as Hiram was, he could kill. *And if I don't try to stop him, I'll be failing Jesus again.*

Matthias turned around and began to run as if to save his own life. *Lord God, I lost Judas. Don't let me be too late for Hiram.* Unacknowledged grief— sorrow for the Judas who once had been his friend—overtook Matthias. It tightened his chest and blurred his vision. Panting, he ran on.

In the midday sun Hiram loitered against a wall across from the main gate of Lemuel's mansion. His uniform set him apart from the crowd, as well as his unusual height. He stared fixedly over the servants and merchants plodding in front of him.

Matthias approached him cautiously, wishing for Cleopas.

Hiram never moved his eyes from Lemuel's gate.

Matthias reached his shoulder. Keeping his voice low and easy, he murmured, "Hiram."

The guard spun around, rigid and ready to strike. His eyes blazed. "What are you doing here?"

Matthias raised his chin and said in a low voice, "I came to talk to you about the Messiah. If you believe in him, you cannot resort to violence."

Hiram's breath quickened. "I don't know what you mean. How did you find me?" he hissed.

Calmer than ever, Matthias coaxed, "Let me tell you more about Jesus . . . about how he loves and forgives his enemies as well as his friends."

"You take me for a fool? God's Law demands justice. If Jesus is from God . . ."

"You're right in saying he came from God. But you must cast off the blindness of our generation. Jesus came to show us God's mercy and to save us from the penalty of the Law."

Perspiration beaded across Hiram's lean face. "How do you know these things?" he asked hoarsely.

Matthias slipped his hand under Hiram's arm and urged, "Leave Lemuel to God. Come with me now and learn about our Messiah and his way." Hiram could have tossed him aside more easily than he'd thrown Cleopas to the ground. Instead the fight went out of him. He permitted Matthias to lead him away.

When they had left Lemuel's mansion far behind, Hiram glanced sideways at Matthias and admitted, "I thought God might forgive me if I meted out justice to Lemuel. After treating Judas and me like beloved sons, he used us like the lowest of slaves."

"Hiram, even Lemuel could be forgiven if he repented and asked for forgiveness."

Hiram frowned. "If you speak the truth, then Iscariot too could have been forgiven and reinstated in the Messiah's favor."

Matthias nodded. With effort he said, "Yes, even Judas could have been forgiven." As he spoke he suddenly realized the worst of his rage at Judas had been rage at himself—at his own guilt. Now that Jesus had forgiven him, he no longer needed to despise Judas.

Aloud he admitted, "Hiram, in our own ways we both betrayed Jesus. I thought I knew what was best for him. I actually thought I knew better than the Son of God!"

"Get out of the road!" shouted an angry merchant, straining to lead his heavily laden donkey past them. The two men gave way and then walked on.

"You were Iscariot's friend," Hiram commented.

"Yes. Whether for good or ill, I loved him," said Matthias. "So did Jesus."

After a long silence, Hiram said humbly, "I owe you my life. How can I ever repay you?"

"You owe me nothing. After all, you saved my life twice."

"Twice? I don't know what you mean."

"By releasing me from that dungeon and then again when you took me from the Romans the day of the crucifixion."

"I didn't rescue you from the Romans. And I've never figured out why Neriah chose to take you from them. Only the day before he was hoping to see you turned into a galley slave."

"Neriah! What are you saying, man?"

"Neriah paid the centurion for his silence and your release. He and his servants carried you to the cheese shop."

Matthias gaped. "But Cleopas said it was you."

Hiram shook his head. "You've got it all confused. I had nothing to do with it. And now this is my home. I must go in and wash before reporting for duty."

Matthias barely heard. The news that Neriah had saved him left him groping for balance as much as if Hiram had slammed him on the chin with his fist.

Twenty-Six

Miriam answered Matthias's pounding on the door.

"You were right about Hiram," he told her. "He was not himself. But I think his reason has returned." As he told her what had happened, he watched the play of emotion on her face. In the end he couldn't tell if it was love or pity. He concluded, "He's safely home now."

"Thank you so much for going after him. I knew you would do something to help him." Her voice quavered and she ran, leaving him at the open door.

Matthias started after her, and then remembering she belonged to Hiram, he reined himself in. To Hannah, who had entered with the baby in her arms, he exclaimed, "Go to her, Hannah!"

"Lately it's better to let her alone," said Hannah. "She'll cry a little and be herself in a few minutes."

He couldn't argue, for he no longer knew what was best for Miriam, and the reason he'd come pressed for attention. "Hannah, Hiram told me Neriah rescued me the day of the crucifixion. Why did Cleopas lie to me?"

She stared at him in surprise and then said slowly, "Neriah made us promise. It seemed safer to obey his wishes. And after all, we owed him something for saving you."

In the upper city, at Neriah's gate, Matthias banged the knocker and identified himself. "I seek audience with your master," he explained to the gatekeeper.

"One moment, sir."

An unnatural silence hung over the mansion. Matthias wished he were anyplace else, yet from the moment Hiram had spoken Neriah's name, he'd known he'd have to come. It was not that he owed his life to Neriah. He owed his life to the Lord, and if he failed to forgive, he'd be stepping into the camp of Iscariot again.

But Lord, Neriah plotted your death and killed Joel and Shebuel and Zibiah. How can I face him and not curse him?

He unclenched his hands and folded his arms and tried to picture himself on a Galilean hill beside Jesus, with a breeze gusting off the lake to cool their faces . . .

How you blessed me long before you became my Lord. Neriah was my friend too . . . until . . . He choked on his condemnation of Neriah, for he, Matthias, had betrayed Jesus, just as Neriah had betrayed him. Then, as clearly as when it had happened, he could see Jesus with scarred hands, offering him bread at Emmaus. The Lord's forgiveness had lifted Matthias from despair. And the Lord had commanded, "Forgive . . . love . . . bless those who curse you."

Suddenly the gate swung wide. Behind the gateman stood Elizabeth, her eyes glistening with tears. "I prayed you'd come. You may be Neriah's only hope." She led him swiftly through the courtyard, down a wide hallway, and to a closed door. With one hand on the latch, she warned, "You won't recognize him." Her lips trembled. "I'd be glad . . . even to see him angry . . ."

Matthias followed her into a richly furnished apartment. At an inner door she called with forced cheer, "Neriah, I bring a guest . . . an old friend." She beckoned to Matthias and entered.

Neriah sat at a long marble-topped table. In front of him lay a wrapped parchment of Scripture and a gold-tipped pointer for following its ancient script, but the Pharisee sat staring into space, his hands limp in his lap, as if he had turned to cold marble himself. He gave no indication he heard his wife.

She went to his side, smoothed his hair, and straightened the folds of his robe as if he were her child, rather than her husband. Matthias stared and then looked away. Even though it was Neriah, he felt embarrassed for the man.

Elizabeth said, "Come over here, Matthias, so he can see you." She placed a chair across the table from Neriah.

Hesitantly, Matthias obeyed. At his approach Neriah, for the first time, showed some sign of life.

"Matthias?" His voice rattled in his throat like the voice of an aged person. Indeed he looked old, for his flesh had wasted away and dark hollows encircled his bleak eyes.

"Yes. It's me," Matthias answered.

Neriah let out a shuddering breath. "I thought you wouldn't come even if I begged . . ."

"You wanted to see me?" Matthias sat cautiously on the edge of his chair. Neriah raised shaking hands to his face and rubbed his eyes, like someone awakening. "Yes." His reply barely reached the ears of his listeners, but it roused Elizabeth to action.

"My husband, I will bring food and wine for our guest." Without waiting for his assent, she hurried away.

To all appearances, Neriah was receiving the retribution Matthias had hoped he would receive. But even as Matthias watched, color began to tint his sunken cheeks, and he began to look more like himself. He croaked, "I wanted to . . . beg your forgiveness. I cannot undo . . . what I've done, but if you could possibly . . . forgive me . . . I could begin . . . to try to atone . . ."

Years of resentment exploded inside Matthias. *God, is that all you're going to ask of him? Just let him say he's sorry and free him, now that he is finally suffering too?*

Neriah reached a shaking hand toward Matthias, but then let it fall to the table beside his unopened scroll. "No," he said. "How can you forgive? If I were you, neither could I." He rocked back and forth with his head bowed. In a barely audible voice he mumbled, "It wasn't a ghost or a vision. I saw him as surely as I see you. He smiled . . . as if I were a friend . . . rather than his executioner."

"You saw Jesus?" Matthias exclaimed in disbelief.

"Jesus!" gasped Neriah, jerking himself straight and staring at Matthias, terrified. "No! No! Joel. I saw Joel."

Clearly Neriah was suffering a just torment. God must be sending a confusing spirit to goad him. Matthias kept silent. After all, what could he say before the hand of God?

Elizabeth and a young serving woman returned, bearing wine and food. They laid the table and provided the men with water for ritual cleansing. After the washing of hands, Elizabeth said, "Please eat with our guest, Neriah." He didn't answer. As she left them, her eyes pleaded with Matthias.

For her sake Matthias said to his immobile host, "I would like to offer the blessing." He offered a brief, traditional prayer and raised his wine goblet. Neriah fumbled to match his gesture. They each sipped a little wine. Then

Matthias handed bread to Neriah. Like an obedient child, he took it and ate.

After a few minutes, in a steadier voice, Neriah said, "You don't believe me . . . that I saw Joel alive again."

"I believe you," Matthias answered, trying to humor him, as he supposed Elizabeth would.

"You lie!" cried Neriah, his voice suddenly strong. "You think a spirit is tormenting me."

Neriah's demeanor made Matthias reconsider. He dropped his hands to his lap, leaned back, and said, "Tell me what you saw."

"I was returning from the Hill of the Skull after the earthquake with two members of the Sanhedrin. We were hurrying to see to our own households, and just inside the city gate where Joel used to meet with those thieves . . ."

Neriah stopped. His lips parted and his eyes widened, as if he were gazing at a terrifying spectacle.

"Yes. What did you see?" Matthias prodded.

Neriah's eyes flicked back to Matthias and focused. "I saw Joel . . . standing with his filthy friends. When he saw me he raised his hand in greeting. I started toward him . . . he stepped back . . . and suddenly only the beggars were there, leering at me. My companions saw Joel too. They asked me who the noble young man was who had waved to me."

"They saw him too?" Matthias caught his breath and then forced himself to speak calmly. "I heard that at the time of Jesus' death some people saw friends and relatives who had been raised from their graves."

"My report is true. If you don't believe me, you can ask my friends."

"But they wouldn't know Joel from any other young man."

"They knew he was different from any man they'd ever seen . . . His countenance . . . He looked wiser than the wisest, and compassionate." Neriah's voice dropped to a whisper. "Like the Nazarene."

He hunched over and hid his face with his hands. "I swear I saw Joel alive again! And after watching Jesus die . . . and seeing Joel . . . I knew . . . I had killed the Promised One."

Neriah rocked in abject misery.

Matthias wanted to shout, "Yes, you murderer!" Instead he simply watched without compassion. At last Neriah knew what he'd done.

Then as if Jesus were in the room speaking, Matthias heard, "I forgave you. Will you withhold my love from him?"

Slowly Matthias stood up and walked around the table.

Neriah, head down, clutching his chest, kept rocking.

Touching his shoulder, Matthias said, "Our Messiah will forgive you. You need only to ask."

Neriah looked up in agony. "I can't believe that. I only pray that I may somehow atone for my sin."

"You can never atone, but the Lord will forgive you."

"I know nothing about forgiveness!" cried Neriah. "All I know is guilt and justice and retribution."

"You asked me to forgive you."

"I said that from my desire, not from any understanding. I know you cannot."

Again resentment overwhelmed Matthias. *Lord Jesus, help me. He speaks the truth. I can't forgive him.*

A quietness from outside himself strengthened him.

"I do . . . forgive you," he blurted, while a tight knot inside him was still screaming no! And when he said the words, forgiveness came like a flood. It staggered him. He tightened his grip on Neriah's shoulder. "I forgive you. Will you forgive me? I want us to be brothers like we once were."

Neriah struggled to his feet and swayed weakly. "Brothers?" he repeated. His eyes filled with tears.

"Brothers," Matthias affirmed, steadying him with a hand on each shoulder.

Neriah grabbed him in a desperate embrace.

The peace Matthias always had felt in the presence of Jesus fell over him. It filled him. He was more healed than when Jesus had healed his useless hand. This, then, was the greater blessing . . . to forgive . . . and to love, as Jesus loves.

Neriah released Matthias and with an agonized expression said, "I've prayed many prayers, yet I know not how to ask forgiveness for betraying the Messiah."

"Yes, you do," Matthias clasped his hand. "You've already said to me what you long to say to God."

"Will you pray with me?"

"Of course."

Standing where they were, they bowed their heads.

Neriah, the eloquent rabbi of the School of Hillel, could only cry, "Oh, God, forgive me!"

Matthias added his own simple plea. "Heavenly Father, for the sake of your Son and our Messiah, please hear the prayer of my brother."

And it was enough. The Pharisee began to weep, like a woman weeps over beauty, or a man, from the joy of first love.

Elizabeth, returning to take away the dishes, appeared in the doorway. "Neriah!" she cried, rushing to her husband.

Neriah caught her in his arms and crushed her to himself. "Elizabeth. Oh Elizabeth. God has forgiven me. Will you forgive me?"

"My dearest, I forgave you long ago. Long, long ago." She clung to him in welcome.

Matthias turned away to grant them privacy.

Because they begged him, Matthias stayed and answered as many of Neriah's questions about Jesus as he could. Then, just before leaving, he said, "Neriah, why did you save my life the day Jesus was crucified?"

"They told you after all, then?"

"I learned it from Hiram."

Neriah frowned thoughtfully. "I'm not sure I can explain it. I was so angry. I'd been up all night, following every word of the trial. I couldn't understand Jesus. At first I thought him stupid.

"Then as he continued to refuse to defend himself, fear began to gnaw at me. And after the scourging, when he shouldered his cross, his eyes met mine . . . and I sensed he knew me . . . not only knew my name, but knew me.

"I felt so unclean. Looking back, I think I began to change then, although I jeered and spat on him with the rest." Neriah shuddered.

"And then you saved me," said Matthias.

Neriah shook his head. "It was Jesus who saved you. His courage and dignity pierced my anger. He made me sick of myself. I knew I'd condemned an innocent man. Following him down the street, I was weary and growing more frightened by the minute. When you burst out of the crowd, I acted without thinking.

"Jesus saved you," Neriah repeated. "And I know now that if it were not for the forgiveness of Jesus, you wouldn't have come to me today. And if you had not come, I would have died . . . by my own hand. So we both owe our lives to the Messiah," Neriah concluded.

Twenty-Seven

By the ninth hour, still lighthearted from the surprise of God's greater blessing, Matthias bounded up the stairs to the room where the Apostles were gathered in prayer.

He knelt at the rear of the group of believers who lingered with the Eleven and added his own silent petition. *Lord God Eternal . . . our Father . . . in my great thanksgiving . . . I possess no worthy offering . . . except the new life you've bestowed on me. Please use me now and forever, according to your own purposes.* It was a brief, groping prayer, but for Matthias it was the most important prayer he'd ever uttered. And through his heart and mind and soul, trust in God flowed like a rushing river, as tangible to him as his healed hand.

In the room around Matthias, praying voices rose and fell until Peter pronounced a final blessing and stood up to address the believers. "Brothers," he said, "you all know how Judas fulfilled the Scripture that one of the Messiah's own men would betray him." Everyone muttered at the mention of the traitor's name.

Peter's leonine face remained calm. He continued, "Scripture also says someone else should take over the estate he abandoned." He spoke carefully and the men listened with respect. "One of the disciples, who was with Jesus from the beginning until the time he left us on the Mount of Olives, should be added to the Eleven to take Iscariot's place."

"Let us consider Joseph bar Sabbas," called Nathanael.

"I say we consider Matthias bar Aaron," suggested Andrew.

Matthias scrambled to his feet. "Please. Not me. I want only to be a servant."

Peter's eyebrows lowered, shading his deep-set eyes. "Do you still misunderstand our calling, Brother? Each believer is called to serve. And the Apostles are to be servants of all." Then he smiled, taking the edge off of his blunt words. "Let the Lord's will be done, Matthias."

Matthias sat down. *Oh, Lord, will I never learn? I will be whatever you want me to be.*

After they prayed the Apostles cast lots in front of the two men. From a jar they shook several short sticks and a long one. The long stick fell against the hem of Matthias's robe, signifying that he was the chosen one. He was an Apostle.

He sat with bowed head. *Lord, help me truly to be a servant to all.*

As if Jesus were whispering in his ear, he heard, "You did not choose me. I chose you. Take my good news to all the world."

Lord, I live to obey. Your will is mine. To my death I will declare your word.

Darkness had enveloped the city by the time Matthias returned to the house of Shebuel. A single torch burned inside his own gate to guide him to his room. He still felt like his feet wore wings and the light of heaven illumined his way.

From across the courtyard Tobias called, "You have a guest, sir." The steward brought a lighted hand lamp to Matthias. "She insisted on waiting for you, so I took her to the guest room."

"She?"

"The lady, Miriam."

"Miriam here?"

"Shall I tell her you've arrived?"

"No. I'll go and announce myself. Thank you, Tobias."

Tobias saluted respectfully and retreated to his own quarters.

Matthias held the flickering oil flame high as he left the courtyard torch-light. Until now he hadn't realized how impenetrable the darkness had become. What would Ethan and Cleopas be thinking at Miriam's absence? And what was Miriam thinking to come here alone?

He rapped on the door so as not to startle her and then strode in. She was standing still as a statue, waiting.

"Shalom, Miriam."

"Shalom, Matthias."

"Do you really wish me peace?" he asked.

"Of course I do."

"Coming here, alone as you are, doesn't bring me peace, nor will it bring you peace if Hiram hears of it."

"Hiram won't mind."

Having her in his house like this, alone and at night, angered Matthias. How could she be so blind to his feelings? Wanting to shock her, he challenged, "Does your young man think I'm in my dotage, so am no threat to the reputation of his bride-to-be?"

Her eyes wavered away from his. "He knows you are honorable."

"He doesn't know me at all," he remarked bluntly. "Before I take you home, tell me why you came."

Her lips parted, but she said nothing. Instead she gazed at him with such love and desire it took his breath away.

He started to go to her, and then stopped himself. *Not again. Never again will I live for me only. If this were in God's will, she would be free to marry me.*

Miriam came within arm's reach and said, "I asked Hiram to free me, and he has released me from my promise."

Incredulous, Matthias repeated, "You just asked and he let you go?"

"Yes. I thought he'd insist on holding me against my wishes, but . . . he really loves me. He said he wanted only what would make me happy. I could hardly bear the look on his face." Her chin trembled.

"If you feel so sad over your freedom," accused Matthias, "perhaps you should return to him."

"Oh, Matthias. It's only because I love you so much that I can feel some of his pain." She held her hands out in an imploring gesture. "If you won't marry me, I will marry no one."

He crushed her to him and kissed her with all the hunger he had tried so long to deny. Together at last. No more days and nights of loneliness. She completed him as God had wanted Eve to complete Adam. He withdrew his lips from hers and sighed. "For so long I dreamed that you would come to me . . . loving me . . . and at last believing as I believed. When you promised yourself to Hiram, I tried to tell myself it would be enough if you just believed in Jesus. But I was lying. I wanted you. Oh, how I wanted you." He kissed her again, tenderly, lightly, keeping his passion in check.

Her arms tightened around his waist. "God meant me for you. I always knew it. Marrying Hiram would have been like dying. But for you I was willing to die."

He kissed her again, reverently—a prayer of a kiss. "I'm not worth dying for, but thank God he has spared us both."

They held each other quietly, savoring the wonder of their love. Finally Miriam murmured dreamily, "What do you suppose the Lord plans for us in his Kingdom now that we are together?"

Matthias gently pulled away from her. "There's something I haven't told you yet. I've been chosen to be an Apostle."

"An Apostle!" The word jolted her out of her private dreams. "What will that mean for us, Matthias?"

He caught her hand, kissed it, and cradled it against his breast. "I don't know, my love, but I must tell you the truth. Remember how you felt when you were willing to die for me?"

She nodded, her eyes wide with fear.

"That's how I feel about the Messiah."

"And will he require your death?" she gasped.

"I cannot say, but to die for a purpose is a gift from God," Matthias said gently.

"No! Don't talk of death!" She pulled away and clapped her hands over her ears. "I won't listen."

He pulled her hands down and held her tightly in his arms. "Miriam, dearest Miriam. Don't fret. I only wanted to prepare you for how much Jesus always will mean to me."

She clung to him, pressing her face against his chest. "I can't bear to think of you dying, even for him!" she cried.

"Don't be frightened," he soothed. "Not even death could keep us apart. Jesus has opened the very doors of heaven for our home."

Some of the tension went out of her. "Is that really so?"

"Really. Because Jesus lives and reigns, we shall live forever with him."

"And nothing can part us ever?"

"Nothing. You won't escape me again, my love. Oh, Miriam," he exulted, "today is but the beginning of the happiness the Lord has planned for us, and all of our tomorrows will bring only more good."

He kissed her and felt the joy of life return to her lips.

Date Due